Milk Teeth
Milchzähne

Copyright © Helene Bukowski 2023,
Originally published in Germany:
Helene Bukowski: MILCHZÄHNE. Roman
© Aufbau Verlag GmbH & Co. KG, Berlin 2019
(Published with Blumenbar; »Blumenbar« is a
trademark of Aufbau Verlag GmbH & Co. KG)
Translation copyright © Jen Calleja, 2023
This English-language translation first published
in the United Kingdom by MTO Press in 2023.

Design by Gabriela Basta-Zabawa
Typeset in Juana, Adobe Garamond Pro
Cover art: treatment of '15.I.1977-1982 (A)' (1977)
by Maria Łuszczkiewicz-Jastrzębska,
image via Zachęta National Gallery of Art,
reproduced under a CC BY-SA licence.

The moral right of Helene Bukowski to be identified as the
original author of this work has been asserted in accordance
with Section 77 of the Copyright, Designs and Patent Act 1988.

The moral right of Jen Calleja to be identified as the
author of this translation has been asserted.

The moral right of the editors has been asserted.

All rights reserved. No part of this publication may be
reproduced, stored in a retrieval system or transmitted
in any form or by any means, electronic, mechanical,
photocopying, recording or otherwise, without
prior permission in writing from MTO Press.

This is a work of fiction. Unless otherwise indicated, all the
names, characters, businesses, places, events and incidents in
this book are either the product of the author's imagination
or used in a fictitious manner. Any resemblance to actual
persons, living or dead, or actual events is purely coincidental.

ISBN 978-1-916913-01-1

MTO Press
Essex County
United Kingdom
mtopress.com

Milk Teeth
Milchzähne

a novel by
Helene Bukowski

translated by
Jen Calleja

— MTO PRESS
WIVENHOE 2023

For Tressow

"Don't you think sometimes people are formed by the landscape they grow up in?"
— JOAN DIDION

Milk Teeth
Milchzähne

—

The fog has swallowed up the sea. It stands like a wall, there, where the beach begins. I can't get used to the sight of the water. I'm always looking for a bank on the opposite side that could reassure me, but there's nothing but sea and sky. These days, even this line is blurred.

We hardly ever see the sun, but that will change. There's a sign already; the animals are losing their colour here now too. Some of them try to escape across the sea, but the waves wash them back up on the beach after a few hours. We find them among the pieces of driftwood and plastic. No one knows if we could get sick from them, but our hunger is greater than our fear.

We can't turn back. Some say there was a fire. The dryness of the forests. A single spark. Unfavourable wind. I imagine a black plain. Ash falling like snow. The horizon unobstructed.

Others claimed the process had been creeping. Bit by bit, everything crumbled to dust.

All we can do is forge ahead.

I can't sleep at night. This is why I've decided to begin my account. The activity should fill the dark hours.

I pushed the table we eat at from the middle of the room up against the window. The glass is steamed up from the inside, but I don't want to stare outside anymore anyway. The floor lamp casts a yellow light into the room. There's electricity here. Maybe there are huge wind turbines standing in the middle of the sea. What do they care if our world has fallen apart. Weather permitting, they'll keep turning.

My notes are laid out before me on the rough tabletop. I haven't looked at them once since we left the territory. I didn't want to have to remember. But now, I can no longer block out the images. I start reading, and everything resurfaces. So clearly, as if I were watching a film. With the help of the notes, I want to put everything that happened in the right order. I will tell it as I experienced it, because it should be my story.

When I'm finished with this account, I'll leave it behind in the table drawer, in the hope that we will begin a new life on the other side of the sea.

1.

I was taught to read and write by Edith. Back then, she still considered me her ally. From one afternoon to the next, we sat on the stained mattress in her room and piled books all around us. Outside the window, the fog veiled the landscape. Next to the bed, the wires of the electric heater glowed, and yet it never really got warm. So that I wouldn't freeze, Edith wrapped me in a blanket and sat close beside me while she opened a book and read to me. Time and time again, she paused, ran her finger along the letters and said them loudly and clearly. With great concentration, I repeated them. Later, she would write down individual words and get me to copy them out in crayon:

HOUSE
DOG
FOREST

Soon, I began finding words by myself:

FOG
MOTHER-OF-PEARL
RUST

Now, looking back, these afternoons seem absurd in their peacefulness.

2.

For a long time, the world beyond our plot didn't exist for me. I built caves out of sheets and hid deep inside the house.

"What you need are books," Edith told me.

They lay about all over the place because Edith didn't see the sense in putting them back on the shelf after reading them. Her clothes were wildly strewn around too. When she got dressed, she went from room to room and picked up whatever she found.

Her jewellery, on the other hand, she kept nice and neat in a wooden box on the vanity table in her room. Every piece was adorned with mother-of-pearl. Mother-of-pearl was completely unheard of in the territory before Edith's arrival, she told me once when I couldn't sleep. "They only wear gold rings set with boar teeth or amber here. I told them that amber comes from the sea, too, but they didn't believe me."

"AMBER – PINE RESIN WHICH, IN A PAST AGE, THE SEA HARDENED INTO AN AMORPHOUS MASS," I read the next day in the natural history book Edith left open for me on the kitchen table.

3.

Two Blue Great Danes lived with us in the house. They didn't have names and only listened to Edith. Every morning, she fed them bark she'd peeled from the firewood.

I thought all dogs were fed this way, until I flicked through a book about pets. I read about CANNED FOOD and OFFAL.

When I showed Edith the page, she laughed. "You can't expect the world to be exactly the same as it is in books."

Whenever Edith went out of the house, the dogs wouldn't leave her side. Even the garden appeared to be a threat to the dogs. I, however, liked it there. There were weeds everywhere. Edith taught me the names of the plants. I especially liked GOLDENROD. They had bright yellow blossoms and grew so high that they towered over me.

We picked the MUGWORT and hung it up to dry out in the living room. The whole house smelled of it.

As soon as the STINGING NETTLES spread too much, Edith tore them up out of the ground. I was never allowed to help her. When she came back into the house, her arms would be red and swollen, but each time she did it, she would act as though she hadn't forgotten her gloves on purpose.

From the stinging nettles Edith made mulch, which she diluted with water and put in petrol cans. She used it to fertilise the soil.

Next to the shed, Edith laid out a potato patch. I helped her with the digging and weeding.

On account of the damp weather, there were a lot of snails. In the evenings, I collected them out of the patch and threw them into a plastic bucket that Edith filled with boiling water. I shook the dead animals over the compost.

In the centre of the garden was a pool. The bright blue tiles, dulled. The water, brackish, we bathed in it anyway. Edith taught me how to swim. I learned quickly. When we climbed back out of the water, our lips would be blue with cold. We warmed ourselves by the fire and Edith read me stories about dark and weighty sea creatures that swam in the ocean.

Time and time again, Edith lay for hours in the wet grass and caught rabbits that had gone astray from the nearby meadows with her bare hands. She knew how to butcher them from a book about small animals. In the last chapter, it described how to rear them. I read it out to her, and the next day we built the hutches. Eighteen square-shaped wooden boxes, six to a row. Edith tasked me with taking care of the animals.

From the black fur of the slaughtered animals, Edith sewed coats. For days on end, she sat at the kitchen table and did nothing else.

After finishing a coat, she would take it and drape it somewhere in the house. The way they lay there made me think of sleeping animals. They watched over me in my dreams.

Edith only wore one of the coats. It was as black as the water in the rain barrel next to the house.

She cut the buttons out of the bones, and it had an enormous hood that Edith pulled down over her face when she went into the garden.

She worked on it every night for weeks. At the time, I didn't know that she did it because she couldn't sleep.

I was there the first time she put it on. Outside, the day was dawning. I stood barefoot on the cold flagstones, shivering.

"Do you like it?" Edith asked, turning in a circle.

I didn't say anything.

Edith grabbed my hand. "It's so thick it could stop gunfire," she said.

I replied: "I almost didn't recognise you."

Edith let go of my hand and sent me back to bed.

4.

"Don't go beyond the brambles," Edith ingrained in me.

This rule didn't apply to her. She went when she thought I was sleeping. Through the window halfway up the stairs, I would watch her drive off in our rusty, white pick-up. On the truck bed would be several containers of mulch. When she came back, there were different containers. I assumed it was petrol. She brought back fresh firewood too. Edith never hurried getting out of the pick-up, she always carried a heavy linen bag in her hand. As she walked back into the house, it would bump against her legs with every step and leave behind bruises.

I knew that it was canned food she'd brought back from her wanderings. I would find them the next day in the pantry. Their labels were less faded than the ones on the others.

I read them so often that I learned them by heart and wrote them on a slip of paper in my room: PEA SOUP, PICKLED GREENBEANS, POTTED MEAT, TOMATO SOUP, PICKLED HAM HOCK, EVAPORATED MILK, RED CABBAGE, SAUERKRAUT, MORELLO CHERRIES, ASPIC.

5.

On some days, it was as if the seagulls were dropping out of the sky. We would find them twisted in the grass, their feathers scorched, and often with enflamed patches on their bellies or on their wing joints. Edith buried the carcasses in our garden. She recited rhymes while she did this, I memorised every single one of them. I could recite them now, but who here still cares about poetry?

These burials were always followed by days when Edith wouldn't get up. While she lay motionlessly on her mattress, neither asleep nor awake, I tried to keep within calling distance of her. I brought her food or painted something for her on the paper napkins I found in the kitchen. When I spoke to her, she didn't respond. On better days, I was permitted to bring her a wet flannel and lay it over her face.

6.

I lost my first tooth, and everything began to change. I was lying in my bed under the covers reading with a torch when the tooth gave way under the pressure of my tongue. I spat it out. Not a drop of blood was clinging to it. It lay in my hand like a pearl. I tried to breathe calmly. That a piece of my own body had simply become detached was dreadful to me. I couldn't make sense of it. Fear bound my chest.

Outside my bedroom door, the dogs began to whine. I called for Edith, but didn't get a response. I left my room with the tooth in my hand. The dogs retreated from me. I found Edith curled up on the mattress. She was staring at the ceiling with a blank expression. I held out my tooth to her, but she didn't react. It was only when I started to cry that she sat up and looked at me.

"Please, just go," she said.

The Great Danes came in from the hallway and pushed me from the room, growling.

I crawled into my bed. I held the tooth in my closed hand and didn't dare move.

The morning came, and nothing had happened. I'd lost nothing, except my tooth. I got up, placed it on the window ledge and knocked on Edith's door, but she didn't let me in. I went downstairs and pulled out the medical lexicon. Back in my room, I put the electric heater next to my bed and sat on the mattress with the book. For the very first time, I read about MILK TEETH. The next day, I left our plot. I didn't want to keep to Edith's rules any longer.

I put on my raincoat and went into the garden. The light was milky through the fog. The moisture lay like a thin film on my skin. I stooped towards a rock we'd found while digging. It wasn't too heavy and sat nicely in my hand. With weak knees, I approached the brambles. The forest behind it looked like a painted backdrop. I fixed my gaze on it and threw the rock. It landed on the other side without making a sound. I had to throw ten more rocks before I dared to push my way through.

The forest stood there as if it had been waiting for me all these years. I studied the bark of the pines, shunted the needles on the ground with my feet, put two pinecones in the pocket of my raincoat and lay, until it got dark, in a hollow between the roots, gazing up into the branches above me.

I understood that I belonged here too and that the landscape beyond the house, beyond the garden, was also made for me.

By the time Edith got back up, I had been in the forest six times. I had lost another tooth and put it in a small tin I'd found in the shed.

I showed them to Edith when she came over to me in the kitchen. Her reaction wasn't what I had expected. She folded her arms over her chest and said, "So you're one of them now."

I looked at her blankly.

"I've never lost a single tooth. You really do take after your father."

It was the first time that Edith had spoken about him.

"My father?" I asked.

Edith waved my question aside.

She went back out again and left me once more alone at the table, where I turned the can in my hands and still didn't understand.

Edith found the two pinecones I'd brought back from the forest. For three days, she kept me locked in the cellar. After she let me back upstairs again, I climbed through an open window and fought my way back into the forest.

Disappearing from the house felt like a heavy rock had been removed from my chest.

The next morning, a dazzling brightness filled my room. I thought it was a dream, but the light endured. I looked out of the window and was shocked by what I saw. The sky over the landscape was blue. Not a cloud in sight, only the sun above the house. It was the first time everything wasn't overcast with fog. I had to close my eyes, it glowed red behind my eyelids.

Squinting, I got dressed and went into the garden. I was only wearing a T-shirt, and yet I wasn't cold. The sky stretched far and wide above my head. I had never been so afraid.

Around midday, the fog drew in once more. And in the night, it was so cold that the top layer of water on the rain barrel froze. I broke off a piece, carried it into the house and put it on the kitchen table. I stayed sitting there until the ice had completely melted and watched the way the water ran off the tabletop.

Not long after, the water began to radically change, and for a long time I believed that I was to blame. I hadn't kept to Edith's rule of not leaving the plot and had disturbed the order of things.

To overcome my feelings of guilt, I started writing these things down. Out from single words came whole sentences. Through these I tried to hold onto what was about to disintegrate: the world as I knew it.

I SAW THE BLUE OF THE SKY, IT LOOKED AS IF IT HAD BEEN HOLLOWED OUT, AND I THINK THAT EVENTUALLY THE HOUSES WILL ALSO STAND LIKE SKELETONS.

7.

Months after that first time I had left the plot, Edith found the sentences I'd written. She stared at the paper for a long time without noticing that I was standing right behind her. I didn't dare breathe.

Finally, she put the slip of paper back as if she'd never found it, and before she could discover me, I snuck back into the hallway.

I knew that it would be necessary to hide these sentences better in future.

From then on, I slipped them underneath a loose floorboard in the upstairs hallway. More were added each day. When I ran out of room, I found new places, always careful that Edith didn't find them.

After a while, I had the feeling that the house was comprised only of my sentences. It seemed as if that they were visible under the surface of things, ready to burst out at any moment.

8.

For the first time in my life, I perceived the house in all its clarity.

The paint was flaking off of the green front door, and the dirt on the overlying arched window with its fanning wooden struts was so thick that no light fell through it.

The grey flagstones in the hallway were sticky. It was always dark in the kitchen, not least because of the oak cabinets and the kitchen sideboard, which was black, almost as if its entire surface were charred. It was only darker in the pantry. I sometimes found Edith in there, touching her hair with her eyes closed or her hands balled into fists and screaming at me as soon as she noticed that I had opened the door.

The disarray began to take on new dimensions. It was worst in the living room, the largest room in the house. Edith had pushed the couch into the middle of the room. It sat obliquely across the well-worn carpet. In many places its beige slipcover was scuffed, as though a large animal had rubbed up against it.

Edith had become accustomed to only sleeping in there. She used a sheet that she never washed as a bedspread. It smelled sour from her night sweats.

The floor was covered in a layer of books. Amongst them were half-empty water glasses and used plates.

Edith always left the small cherry wood dresser next to the door open. Its contents varied. Dirty laundry, mason jars, crumpled paper, firewood.

One time, Edith cleared it out completely and only put a brooch up on its shelf. When I entered the room around midday, sunlight fell through the small gap between the curtains and was thrown back onto the walls by the brooch. Scattered light reflections I momentarily mistook for bullet holes.

Sometimes, I went into the cellar out of choice. The entrance was in the hallway. A hatch door, beneath which was a steep, musty wooden staircase leading down into the darkness. The shelves were filled with our provisions. Preserved fruit and vegetables. Dried fruits. Evaporated milk. Rusks. A few of the canned goods Edith had brought back. I found it comforting to count the available supplies. And even when the light from the bulb hanging from the low ceiling went out sometimes, it didn't bother me. I even liked standing in the dark, where it made no difference whether I had my eyes open or shut.

A wide wooden staircase led from the hallway to the upper floor. Its wooden handrail smooth and slinky. Halfway up the stairs was a small window from where we could see the street the house was connected to via a sandy path.

I once startled Edith while she was standing on the stairs and staring out of the window. When she noticed me, she spun around and said: "When they come, I'll stand there and blow them away," then she formed her left hand into a gun. "Bang, bang" she said, aiming at me.

In her room, Edith had covered all her windows in newspaper. She had painted over the thin pages with black shoe polish. From then on, it looked as if she had sealed up the windows with tar.

The bare mattress and quilt were adorned with sweat and blood stains. I surveyed them with the torch.

"No one will ever get them out," Edith said, standing in the doorway. I drew back. She came in and ran her finger over the outlines. "This is my body's inscription. The mattress will always be a monument to me."

She laughed soundlessly and left me once more alone with the trembling beams of the torch.

Edith had wheeled her dented silver roller suitcase next to the bed. Arranged like a relic. She never moved it. I didn't want to disturb it under any circumstances.

Opposite the bed was Edith's vanity. The more time that passed, the dustier it became. The mirror was covered in a thick layer. My face looked like a mask in it.

On its marble top were Edith's lipsticks, a mother-of-pearl compact and a brush made of driftwood, which she used to use to comb her sun-bleached hair for hours.

Sometimes I would hide one of these objects, push the brush under the rug or place a lipstick on top of the wardrobe. It was only when Edith had given up looking that I would let them reappear again.

I also started removing the wallpaper, but Edith didn't mind.

"Some days I'd like to be naked too," was all she said.

Edith's wardrobe took up a whole wall of her room. The mirrored doors made the room look twice its size. Not a single piece of clothing hung from the silver hangers anymore.

When I opened the wardrobe doors, they moved and jingled in the draft of air. Edith had covered the inside walls with pictures of the sea:

SANDY BEACH
BRIGHT DUNES
WASHED UP SEAWEED
MOSSY BREAKWATERS
A PIER IN THE FOG
A BOMBED-OUT BOARDWALK

She only went in the room in order to sit inside the wardrobe and look at the pictures with the torch. If she heard me walking past, she would call out: "I only recognise the pine forest. It looks like the pine forest near the coast."

Next to Edith's room was the bathroom. Dark blue tiles. Many of them cracked. A crack ran across the ceiling too. In the middle of the room was the freestanding bathtub in which Edith was always bathing. Sometimes she forgot to turn off the tap. I was constantly occupied with rushing in, turning it off and mopping up the water that had already flowed over the edge of the bath with towels.

One time, one of Edith's books fell off the sink into the water, maybe I had grazed it with my elbow by accident. It was immediately soaked, swollen. Edith pulled it out, clutched it to her chest and in a flash had grabbed a stone from the edge of the bath that I'd brought out of the forest and placed there. I was able to duck just in time. The stone crashed into the mirror right above me, and a large piece broke off and shattered on the floor.

"That will bring the worst bad luck," I told her, but Edith didn't hear me. She had submerged herself and held her breath until I had left the bathroom.

Edith had blocked up the other rooms with furniture. Much of it was covered with white sheets. Hulking forms. As if this house actually belonged to other people, on whose return we were waiting.

During Edith's sleepless nights she shoved the wardrobes and dressers over the floorboards for hours on end. Traces of this could be seen on all of the walls and on the floor. She was always in search of a different arrangement. I couldn't get used to anything.

From my room, located on the upper floor like Edith's, I moved into the attic. It was the only place I felt safe. She never figured out where I had hidden the wooden pole needed to fold down the ladder.

Up there, it was always a lot warmer than the floors below, so I left the furniture where it was. The mattress beneath the only window. A small writing desk against the other wall. A wide wicker chair opposite it. My clothes, carefully piled in cardboard boxes against the wall. Nothing lay strewn around.

When I opened the window in the evenings, I could smell the pine forest.

Ever since Edith felt betrayed by me, she barely went into the garden.

I created a tunnel system through the brambles. That way I could hide there all day long without having left the plot. Edith barely made any effort to look for me. Often, she would only step out of the front door and call my name. It sounded like she was trying to call in an animal.

Sometimes she would half-heartedly prod a stick into the long grass. I watched her and stayed where I was.

There was only one time when Edith was stubborn. She endured a whole afternoon outside, standing motionlessly in the last of the fog and listening out for a sound from me, while the wetness gathered on the see-through raincoat she wore over her black rabbit fur coat. I crawled so deep into the brambles that the thorns scratched my arms and legs. The scars are still visible. They form a light pattern of fine lines on my skin.

The brambles hardly ever bore blackberries anymore. When they did, I had to give up my hiding place as Edith would notice them immediately and spend the day picking the fruit. She would eat nothing else. The juice dyed her lips, teeth and her tongue dark, almost black.

9.

Ever since it began getting hotter, the rabbits' fur started changing. Every new litter was lighter than the one before, until they were all white, like snow. They had red eyes and were not as strong.
    Edith called them: ALBINO.

I will never forget the way the pelt rotted on the compost, the flies and the stench, because Edith refused to use the white pelt.
    "The colour can't mean anything good," she said.

Other kinds of animals lost their colour too. Suddenly there were only white hens, white horses. A couple of dogs, as if whitewashed. A white fox appeared in the forest. Around the same time the native birds disappeared. I built and hung up nesting boxes for many years in a row, yet every year they remained empty.

Edith no longer took care of the potato patch. I began to make the mulch myself. So that the plants would be able to handle the unending heat, I fertilised them daily. The return was poor. Three times a year I gathered the potatoes from the dry ground and put them in the cellar in a wooden crate, turned the soil and planted new seed potatoes.

I rarely stayed in the house. Instead, I familiarised myself with the landscape.

"You look like them," Edith screeched when I came back from my wanderings and lay my red raincoat, which I had found somewhere in the undergrowth, over the back of a chair.

"I am one of them," I replied, and Edith tried to tip the boiling water from the stove over me. I took cover behind the table. Edith dropped the pan, the water poured over the floor. I climbed onto a chair.

"Traitor," Edith said, and left.

She only left our plot to walk into the forest to fetch a pine branch. Back in the house she would put it in the living room in one of the water glasses and would sniff it every time she walked past.

She didn't drive the pick-up anymore, and new canned goods didn't come.

She barricaded herself deep in the house. Sometimes she lay for days in the bathtub. When she came out, her skin was white and puffy.

At some point I began to hope that Edith would disappear. I dreamt about it over and over.

AN ABANDONED RABBIT FUR COAT SLIPPING HALFWAY OFF THE STAIRS. NO DUST IN THE PLACE WHERE THE SUITCASE USED TO BE. CLEAR OUT THE HOUSE LITTLE BY LITTLE. I STACK FURNITURE IN THE GARDEN AND LIGHT IT, I HEAR THE CRACKLING OF THE WOOD IN THE EMPTY ROOMS.

When I woke up, everything was still there. Her clothes, her jewellery, the pieces of driftwood, the silver roller suitcase and Edith herself, sleeping on the sofa.

The years went by, and I no longer believed that anything more would change. Then I found the child.

10.

I walked through the forest. The pines stood in the last of the light. Time and time again I paused, tilted my head back and looked up at the branches that cut up the sky with their rusty tone. I orientated myself with the markings I had made an age ago. Crosses made in the bark with a knife. The resin had made my fingers stick together. The scent had stayed on my skin for days afterwards.

I reached the clearing. An almost circular zone. Up from the ground grew grasses bleached by the sun. I slowly went into the centre, where I had built branches into a den. It had been my first hiding place in the forest. Far enough away from Edith that I could talk myself into believing that she didn't exist.

Stooping over, I entered through the opening. I saw that the wooden crate that I'd hidden here had been moved. Beside it was a bed made of moss. It smelled differently too. Someone had been here.

I opened the crate, nothing was missing. I took out one of the cigarettes and lit it. When I turned around, standing in front of the entrance was a child. We looked at each other. It was wearing a t-shirt that went down to its knees. Its feet were in oversized trainers, crusted with dirt. But the most remarkable thing was its hair. Red, as if ablaze. No one had hair that colour in the territory. I stepped out of the den, the child backed away.

"What are you doing here?" I asked, lowering the hand holding the burning cigarette.

Without saying anything the child walked past me, sat on the moss bed and wrapped its arms around its knees.

I crouched down in front of the den.

"You can't stay here," I said.

The child turned its head and furtively wiped its eyes. I stepped away from the entrance, it got up and came back outside. It looked around indecisively and fumbled with the hem of its t-shirt. I took a drag on my cigarette. The smoke was barely visible.

With its shoulders hunched, the child went to the edge of the clearing. Once there, it turned around and nodded. It was only once it had disappeared amongst the trees that I understood that the nod wasn't meant for me. The child had bid farewell to the clearing, just like I did every time.

"Come back," I said, raising my voice.

Nothing stirred. I called out again. The pines crackled in the wind. I stepped anxiously from one foot to the other. I was going to shout out a third time, when the child appeared again between the trees. It looked at me, waiting. I stubbed out the cigarette and stuck the butt in the pocket of my raincoat.

"Do you want to come with me?" I asked. The child threw a look back into the forest. The darkness already stood behind the trees. Above us, the sky was losing its colour.

"I live in a house, not far from here. It's safer there."

The child leaned against the pine it was standing next to. I held out my hand. To my surprise it stepped out from the trees.

"Promise?" it asked.

I nodded.

The child took my hand.

"This way. It's not far from here."

While we walked to the house, the child didn't let go of my hand once. If someone had stood in our way, I would have knocked them down without thinking twice.

"You've lost your mind." Edith said.

She stood in the doorframe wearing her black rabbit fur coat. Her greasy hair hung in front of her face. The dark circles under her eyes were dark violet, like bruises. She hadn't got up from the sofa in weeks.

"Where did it come from?" she asked, eyeballing the child, which I had sat on the kitchen table.

"I found it in the forest."

"How can that be?"

I shrugged my shoulders. Edith stood next to me.

"None of the others have hair like that," she said, "it can't be from here."

"How did you make it to this territory?'" she asked the child. As she didn't receive an answer, she turned back to me.

"Can it speak?"

I nodded.

"What are you going to do now?"

"It has to eat something."

"And then?"

"What do you mean?"

"When are you taking it back?"

"Back where?"

"Back to the forest?"

There was a silence.

"I promised it that it can stay with us," I said.

"You did what?"

"I promised it – "

"You really have lost your mind."

"Anyone else would have done the same thing."

Edith twisted her mouth into a sneer.

"You don't really believe that, do you?"

She turned to the child and asked it its name.

Once again, she didn't receive an answer.

"And you're sure it can speak?"

"Before, in the forest – "

"Meisis," said the child, pointing at itself.

Edith shook her head. "Sounds made up."

"I'm called Skalde," I said. I looked at Edith, to prompt her. She cleared her throat and said her own name.

"Skalde, Edith," Meisis repeated. We nodded. The light over our head flickered. I looked at the window. The darkness had swallowed the garden. The kitchen was reflected in the windowpane. Edith and I, shoulder to shoulder, the child shielded by our bodies. We were standing very straight, like we weren't afraid.

I now ask myself whether everything had already been decided in this moment. Had I not already surmised how this would turn out?

I shook my head, took a tin of evaporated milk from the pantry, opened it and poured half into a glass for Meisis.

"You can drink it," I said, passing it to her. Meisis brought it up to her mouth and took a sip. She wanted to give some to Edith, but she ignored her.

"I will most definitely not be bringing up another child, despite objections," she said.

"Are you talking about me?"

Edith nodded.

I laughed.

"Are you really saying that you brought me up?"

Edith took a step back. She had restored the usual distance between us. I waited for her to respond, instead she turned around, left the kitchen and closed the door behind her.

I could physically feel the silence that followed. It lay

across my shoulders and my neck and tightened my muscles. From there, the pain grew right up to my ears. I started at the sound of a fly coming in through the window and buzzing. It bounced off the glass multiple times from the inside, tumbled and fell. Its black body twitched, then it was silent.

"You'll get used to it Meisis," I said, not knowing what I meant. The child nodded and drank another sip of the milk.

I stood up and closed the window. Outside, the darkness was now absolute. I leant my forehead against the glass and closed my eyes.

While I washed up, the child slept on the kitchen table. Their head protectively buried in their arms.

"Come on, I'll take you up to bed," I said, drying my hands on the washcloth. I still remember how I marvelled at how naturally these words passed my lips. As if it wasn't the first time that I had said something like that. I lifted Meisis from the table and carried her upstairs to the attic. There I took off her trainers and lay her on the mattress, where she immediately went back to sleep.

I lay awake for a long time.

Time and again I turned my head and looked at the child in order to make sure that I hadn't just made the whole thing up.

In the early hours I woke with a start. It was as if I hadn't slept. Every muscle in my body hurt. I stretched, but it didn't help much, I couldn't find my way back into sleep, so I got up, sat in the gable window and stared out of it. Outside, nothing had changed.

MAYBE I LOST MY BALANCE A LONG TIME AGO.

11.

I set up a room for the child on the first floor next to the landing. Edith had always discarded things there. Predominantly used crockery. I brought the gold-rimmed plates and cups back to the kitchen by the basketful. A small sofa bed with a blue cover was the only piece of furniture in the room. I brought in a dresser from the hallway. I rolled a swivel chair that had been sitting unused in the cellar up to the window.

"Right," I said to the child. "You can stay here."

She went to the window and looked out. I stood behind her. We could see the garden and the forest. I couldn't find anything remarkable in the view, yet Meisis didn't look away. It was only when I carefully touched her shoulder that she turned back to me.

"This is a good room," she said.

I also showed Meisis the rest of the house. We went in all the rooms. Sometimes she touched the walls, as if she wanted to feel what was underneath the wallpaper.

"Have you always lived here?", she asked me, pushing her hand inside mine.

"Always," I replied.

"I like that, never changing place," she said.

I didn't know how to respond.

In the evening, I asked the child if she would like to have a bath. I showed her the bathroom, and she agreed. I heated water and filled the bathtub to the top. It was so hot that the windows steamed up. I helped Meisis out of her clothes, and she climbed in. From the windowsill I passed her a dish holding the soap I had made from ash and the fat from the rabbits. Meisis washed her arms and legs with it and removed the layer of dirt from her skin.

"Hair too?" I asked. Meisis nodded. I picked up the porcelain beaker from the sink, filled it, instructed her to lean back her head, and emptied it over her. Then I took some of the soap and rubbed it into her hair. I told her that she should keep her eyes closed while I filled the beaker again and washed out the soap. I paused in motion, taken aback. I remembered that Edith had washed my hair the exact same way. I had intuitively taken on her hand movements. It hurt that I had almost forgotten the tranquil moments we'd had with one another.

Meisis gave me a querying look.

"Close your eyes again, I'm not quite finished yet," I said quickly, and washed the remaining soap from her hair.

After the bath I wrapped Meisis in a towel and carried her to her room. I tilted open a window. I could hear the insects outside. A moth bumped against the glass.

"Sleep now," I told Meisis, covering her. As I was leaving the room, she reached her hand out towards me.

"Stay?"

I accepted her request without hesitation.

I still know now that in that moment I thought: so now a child. I didn't question my decision. Nor did I think of the consequences my actions would lead to. All that I concentrated on was the situation I found myself in that moment. To wake up next to the child and hold her hand, as if I had never done anything else.

12.

AGITATED INSIDE. AS IF A HAND HAD DUG INTO ME AND SHIFTED MY GAZE. I STAND STILL, AND IT FEELS UNLEARNED, AFTER ALL THESE YEARS.

I ran through the house the next day like a lunatic, establishing order. In some places the dust lay so thickly I could sink my hand into it. I went into the rooms I hadn't been in for a long time and tried to make them accessible again. Meisis followed me and watched how I gathered clothes and washed them, piled up Edith's books, cleaned the windows, mopped the floors and removed the sheets from the furniture. The house suddenly regained its shape. My movements, too, were more precise.

Edith made no comment.

13.

Our days gained a clear structure. I woke Meisis every morning and we ate a thin broth together.

The heat outside was still bearable in the mornings, and we spent this time in the garden. Meisis played in the long grass, while I watered the potato patch, weeded or fertilised the soil. I often stopped to reassure myself that Meisis was still there. If I didn't see her, I immediately called her name. Back then I already lived in the constant fear that something could happen to her.

Time and again Meisis would interrupt her game, come running over to me and urge me to put out my hand and close my eyes. When I opened them again, she had placed something inside it for me. A stone that she had found, or a small bunch of flowering weeds. I took all these things up to the attic and saved them in a cardboard box that I'd found under the sofa. Nothing in it could be lost.

So that Meisis wouldn't get sunburnt, I built an elaborate construction from sticks and sheets, which increased the shade in the garden. Despite this her skin in the first few weeks was often reddened. At night she complained of pain, I couldn't do anything more than make her cold compresses and sit by her bed.

After a while, Meisis's skin got used to the sun, and a great weight fell from me.

While tidying up I found a box of building blocks I used to play with. Cubes of wood, painted different colours. I still clearly remembered how I had built walls in the hope that

Edith wouldn't be able to climb over them. But she was able to bring them down with a single kick.

I carried the building blocks into the garden for Meisis, and she occupied herself for a time with nothing else. Instead of using them for building, like I'd shown her, she spent hours sorting them. I never worked out her ordering system.

I tied large cloths around her head to protect her against the sun. Even the dark blue one didn't conceal the colour of her hair. The red always shimmered through.

When I did the washing, Meisis wanted to do it too. As soon as I put the silver-coloured tin tub on the table in the garden and filled it with boiling water, she came bounding over like a puppy, almost tumbling, and would hang off of my leg. I put a footstool next to me so that she could dunk her arms into the water too. She tried to copy my movements and helped me to wring everything out and hang it on the washing lines I had stretched between the plum tree and the cherry tree.

I liked nothing more than the scent of the suds that hung in the air after doing the washing. Meisis was no different. Sometimes she lay between the sheets and stayed there until everything was dry.

Just before the sun was at its peak, we went back into the house. I would often lay down for a nap, and Meisis would doze too. Most of the time she picked up her blanket and made herself comfortable between the dogs that lay in the corridor on the cold flagstones. When she slept there I didn't worry, because the dogs protected Meisis as if she were one of their young.

We would spend the afternoon in the house. I tried to keep the rooms in order, mopped the floorboards, piled the books and folded the clothes. Meisis helped me or resumed her game that she had begun in the garden with the building blocks inside.

Sometimes I put a glass of water next to the sofa for Edith. She didn't thank me, but when I came back into the living room a few hours later, I saw that she had drunk from it. I heard her sometimes walking through the house, only at night, restless, like in the years previous.

In the evenings I cooked something from the provisions that we still had and ate with Meisis in the kitchen. We mostly ate in silence, yet I liked this hour of quiet. Even the dogs seemed to like it, because they always came and slept peacefully under the table.

When the sun started to go down, we went back into the garden and I watered the potato patch and the mulberry bush, even though I couldn't remember the last time it had carried fruit. The smell of the wet earth reminded me of the time of the fog. Sometimes I stood in the garden until it was dark. Meisis, all the while, never leaving my side.

We took care of the rabbits together. Meisis gave every animal a name, but I could never memorise them.

Meisis was present when I butchered one of the rabbits for the first time after her arrival. I showed her the individual steps. She didn't look away and intently watched every one of my hand movements. She understood that we relied on the animals' meat.

After she had watched a few times, she already knew how to do it and asked me to let her do it herself.

Every evening I sat next to Meisis's bed until she was asleep, all the while looking out of the window at the tops of the pines, which I could make out in spite of the darkness.

WITH THE CHILD IN THE HOUSE THE NIGHTS HAVE BECOME BRIGHTER. THE DARKNESS IS NOW SOFT LIKE A COAT MADE OF FUR. I LAY IT ABOUT MY SHOULDERS.

14.

CROUCHED IN THE OPEN LANDSCAPE, YOU WOULD STILL NOT BE INVISIBLE, FOR HERE THEY HAVE LEARNED TO NOTICE ABNORMALITIES EVEN WITH THEIR EYES CLOSED.

I forbade Meisis from using the front door and only allowed her to play behind the house, because no one could see into the garden from the road.

When she asked me why, I said "It's safer there."

15.

I SLEEP AS IF SOMEONE HAD KNOCKED ME
UNCONSCIOUS, THE DARKNESS DRAWS CIRCLES, I SINK
DOWN BETWEEN THEM.

I can't remember a single dream from these first few weeks. It was as if my body was completely focused on filling all energy reserves in order to steel itself for what was still to come.

I awoke every morning even before the sun was in the room. In the hours that followed I moved aimlessly through the house. Sometimes I would open Meisis's bedroom door. She always slept peacefully, her body relaxed. But once she was lying strangely curled up, and in her hair I found dried out pine needles, as if she had just run through the forest.

When I looked in her room again a short while later, she lay like she always did and the pine needles were gone. I thought that I'd just imagined the whole thing.

16.

I barely saw Edith in those first few weeks. She didn't seem to even notice that Meisis was living in the house with us. She continued to mostly sleep on the sofa. Or she withdrew into the bathroom, where she spent hours lying in the bath.

But once, while I was sitting in the garden with Meisis, I had the strong feeling that she was watching us through one of the windows. I looked at the house, but all the curtains were closed and nothing confirmed my suspicions.

"Has Edith ever been different?" Meisis asked me once during supper, while she mashed a potato with her fork. I told her that Edith had been behaving like that for a long time.
    Then Meisis wanted to know why Edith never ate with us. I explained to her that Edith preferred to do without food.
    "But how does she survive?"
    I said: "Not everything can be explained logically." I didn't want to talk about Edith anymore.

17.

I DREAMT THE SMELL OF GUNPOWDER. THE LAND HAS BEEN LEFT FULL OF HOLES. I FALL IN THE BLANKS.

The dogs wrenched me from my sleep. Their barking sounded hoarse. I peeled myself, dazed, from the sweaty sheet that I used for a cover and went downstairs.

The dogs stood yapping in the corridor. I tried calming them, when I noticed that the front door was ajar. I slowly went over to it and put my hand on the doorknob. Through the narrow gap I could see a section of the path. Its reflection of the sunlight was dazzling. I pushed open the door and stepped outside.

In the middle of the sand track that led to the road stood Meisis. The sunlight ignited her hair, she had turned away from the house so that I couldn't see her face.

I grabbed her and pulled her back into the house.

"What were you doing in the front garden?" I shouted.

Meisis said nothing. She looked at me frightened. Only now did I notice that she was holding a tin pressed to her chest.

"Have you forgotten that you're not allowed to play in the front garden?" I asked. "Someone could have seen you. Only the house and the garden are safe, do you understand?"

Meisis seemed not to have heard me, her eyes were fixed on the can.

"The tins aren't for playing with," I explained to her.

Meisis nodded.

"It's best if we stay in the house today," I said and pushed her into the kitchen.

I closed the curtains, put the can back in the pantry and

took a jar of preserved cherry plums off the shelf. It gave a loud crack when I opened it. I put the jar in front of Meisis on the table. She grabbed it with both hands.

"You can drink the juice," I told her and passed her a fork for the fruit. Meisis put the jar up to her mouth and took a sip.

"Sweet," she declared.

I let her have the whole jar and only ate a rusk.

18.

The child and I were spending the morning in the garden when an incident occurred. Meisis was crouching in the long grass sorting building blocks, and I was sitting in the plum tree picking dry leaves from the branches, when there was a movement in the forest. I immediately climbed down and stood with my legs apart in the grass. Meisis noticed the change in atmosphere. From the corner of my eye, I watched as she slowly lowered her hand holding the brick and gradually directed her gaze between the trees, too.

I was going to shout something, but I couldn't release my tongue from the roof of my mouth. Something was stuck in my throat, immobilizing me. Then I saw that it was Kurt standing in the forest. We looked at one another. He put his finger to his lips and the next moment he was gone. I swallowed.

Meisis stood next to me and pushed her hand into mine.
"Was someone in the forest?" she asked.
"Go inside please," I said.
Meisis nodded and walked inside.
I stayed in the garden and waited, but Kurt didn't allow himself to be seen a second time.

THE FOREST IS DIFFERENT. MAYBE THE TREES HAVE BEEN SWAPPED OVERNIGHT, AND NOW THERE ARE FAKES STANDING THERE INSTEAD, WHOSE ONLY FUNCTION IS TO BE HIDING PLACES TO OPTIMISE THE AMBUSH.

19.

The books in the house used to belong to Kurt. He lived on the ground floor of the prefab high-rise next to the river. The other apartments were empty. There were marks on the carpets and the walls where the furniture used to be. Bright spots which accented the absence of things. Even back then Kurt had barely owned anything. A thin foam mattress, a blanket, a folding stool and a reading lamp. And the books. They were piled up in all of the four rooms and formed precarious towers, between which only small paths remained to go from one room to the other.

Kurt spent his days reading on the mattress, or he spent hours in the forest without a concrete destination.

One night there was a short circuit in one of the upper floors, and a fire broke out. Kurt brought his books to safety and watched from the riverbank how the fire blazed in the windows and burned up the rooms inside.

No one noticed the fire, and by the morning it was too late. Only a sooty ruin remained.

Kurt refused to move into another house and decided to live in the forest.

"I had never met anyone as fearless as your mother," Kurt told me, "and she was heavily pregnant." The admiration he showed for her was real. It was as if he was talking about someone else.

Kurt gave Edith all of his books in exchange for a rabbit fur coat and the promise that he could come by at any time to read them.

"I knew from Nuuel how much she loved to read. I wouldn't have wanted to give my books to anyone else."

When I saw Kurt for the first time, the fog was still so thick that his range of vision was limited to only a few meters. Edith let him in the house and was about to take him straight to the books, but he stayed where he was, crouched down in front of me and held out his hand. His gaze was frank.

"I hope that you're making it easier for her," he said, so quietly that only I heard it. At the time I didn't know what he meant by it. But I understood that was something important, something significant.

I found the high-rise years later. With its greyness and austerity, it seemed as unreal as the pool in our garden. All the windowpanes were broken. I found a stained mattress that someone had thrown in the elevator shaft. Birch trees were growing on the ground floor, and I imagined how they would soon bring down the building.

20.

"Where did you come from?" I asked Meisis one evening.

We ate the leftover rabbit from the day before. Meisis had watched me for a long time, how to gnaw the bones so that they would shine like they were polished.

She wiped her mouth and put the bone she was holding in her hand in front of her on the plate and looked at me as if she hadn't understood my question.

I leaned over the table. "You can tell me," I said, and gave her the last piece of rabbit.

Meisis looked at the meat, hesitated and shook her head.

I sighed.

"Will someone be missing you?" I asked. "Can you tell me that?"

Meisis seemed to consider it; she picked a piece of gristle from the bone, then said: "No, no one." She put the gristle in her mouth and chewed.

I leaned back and thought about pushing the plates from the table suddenly, but the door opened and Edith came in. She stumbled over to the kitchen sink, picked up the jug and poured water over her wrists.

Meisis put down her bone and looked at her. "Yesterday someone was standing in the forest," she said. Edith turned to us.

"Who?" she asked me.

"Kurt," I replied shortly.

"And he didn't want to come in the house?"

I said no.

"Odd," Edith said, shaking the water from her hands.

"Other people live around here?" Meisis wanted to know.

I bit my lip. Edith laughed shrilly.

"Better if you don't meet them," she said. Meisis rumpled her forehead. I didn't tell her anything more either.

I got up, took Meisis' bone from the plate and cleared away the plates in the sink. I gnawed off the remaining meat from the bone while standing and lay it like a good luck charm on the windowsill.

OUR SILENCE HAS TWICE THE WEIGHT.

21.

I woke with a start. It took some time before I found my way out of the dream and back into reality. I tried to bring the room around me into focus. Sunlight lay in a bright square on the floorboards. The air smelled of dry wood. I knew that I would have to leave our plot that day. I had put it off for too long. I got dressed, my heart throbbing.

I told Meisis that she would have to stay in the attic all day. I sat her down on my mattress and put three cartons of evaporated milk next to her.
"Don't move from here under any circumstances, you hear me?" I said.
Meisis wrapped her arms around her knees.
"But where are you going?"
I put my hand on her head.
"It won't take long."
Meisis asked if she could come too. I said no.
"You stay here. When I'm downstairs, close the hatch, understand?"
Meisis nodded.
I stroked her hair and climbed down.

The pick-up wouldn't start until the third attempt. It was so hot I had to keep wiping my brow so the sweat wouldn't run in my eyes. I drove along the road slowly. It cut straight through the overgrown fields. To the left and right stood chestnut trees, their leaves brown and dry. They would instantly crumble to dust in your hand. The sunlight threw their shadows in patterns on the asphalt.
Len and Gösta's house was up on a hill. The road led

directly to it. I parked the pick-up in the driveway. Gösta's salmon faverolle hens scratched at the dry ground in the front garden. None of them still possessed the colour of their name. Instead, they were as pale as the whitewashed house.

Underneath the blooming elderflower bush near the fence, Len was sitting on a plastic chair. She was wearing her sunglasses and had her arms crossed over her faded nightshirt. I went over and crouched down beside her.

"Is that you, Skalde?" she asked. I offered my face to her, so she could examine it with her hands.

To this day I still remember the story of how Len was blinded. It happened long before I was born, and yet she had told me so many times, it seemed as if I had been there. It was the first cloudless day in years, the temperature was below freezing. Len had climbed up a hill in rubber boots. The frozen earth cracked under her soles. She was standing right at the top when, suddenly, the sky grew dark, though it was only noon. The whole horizon reddened like the sun was setting. Astonished, Len raised her head and stared at the sun, which was obscured by a black moon. She was so fascinated by what was happening, she didn't look away for minutes on end. The sky regained its colour, and she squinted. A white spot appeared in her line of vision, burnt up, and all that remained was darkness. When they found her, she was blind in both eyes.

"You well? Is it bearable with Edith?" Len asked.

"She sleeps a lot," I replied.

Len placed a hand on my shoulder. "You have the heaviest heart. It's never been easy for you."

"Are you going to come and visit me again soon?"

"I'd like to very much, but I lose my way in this heat."

I didn't say anything.

"Maybe we just have to make the best of it, it's out of our hands," she added.

"Let's go in," I said, helping her up and leading her inside. The window shutters were closed. It was pleasantly cool. Through the open living room door, I could see Gösta. She was sitting forlornly on the sofa. It looked like her wrinkled skin was covered in a coating of dust. Only the flickering of the television illuminated the room.

"Go in quietly," Len said. Maybe she had sensed my hesitation. She squeezed my hand and slowly walked in the direction of the kitchen, feeling along the wall as she went.

I took a breath and entered the living room. Gösta didn't move. I sat down next to her on the worn leather sofa. The greyish carpet was so thick, my shoes sank into it.

The television showed a jittery shot of the river. The strong waterflow kept loosening rocks from the banks and pulling them into its depths. The sky was shrouded by clouds. It was drizzling.

"Had to cover the camera with a plastic sheet, otherwise the rain would have ruined the electronics," Gösta said, without unfixing her gaze from the television.

The camera's image stablised. The sight of the dark water made me sleepy. I propped myself up on the armrest.

"No one can even imagine now that the weather was always like that," Gösta said. The shot now showed a road, half submerged in fog. The asphalt was broken in a lot of places. Beneath it lay the old cobblestones. Rain had collected in the potholes.

"But it'll be like that again," I said insistently, pointing at the television. Gösta took off her glasses and polished them with the hem of her nightshirt.

"It has to. Anything else is frankly no way at all. I never

knew temperatures over twenty degrees when I was a child. I slept under the skylight, and every night I'd hear the rain. Now I lie in bed and can hardly move it's so hot. It's enough to drive you mad." She put her glasses back on and looked at me. "But I always say to Len, we have to be patient. Summer can't last forever."

I nodded. I too had talked myself into believing that it was only a matter of time before the fog returned.

I could now see Gösta's and Len's house in the video. It was flanked by bare birch trees. It took a moment before I realised that it wasn't dust, but hoarfrost that covered the branches. Len stepped out of the front door. Inside her rubber boots she was wearing thick socks, which she had pulled up to just below her knees. A scarf and hat concealed her face. She stretched her hand out into the air. Fine snow was falling from the sky. A metallic clicking sound came from the video-recorder, and a black and white flickering replaced the picture.

Gösta rubbed her eyes.

"Shall we?" she said, getting up from the sofa. Without first switching off the television, she went outside. I followed her into the garden.

We walked along the dry-stone wall until the end of the plot, where the vegetable patch was in a shady hollow. The beds were protected from the hens with a picket fence.

"It all needs watering," Gösta said.

She sat on the bench under the blooming apple tree, and I went to the shed and fetched the watering can. I filled it from the pump next to the house and, careful not to spill anything, carried it to the vegetable patch.

I had to go to the pump a dozen times before all the beds were watered enough. Drenched in sweat, my t-shirt clung to my back. I put the watering can back in the shed and sat down next to Gösta on the bench. A gust of wind drifted through the branches. White blossom fell all around us. Gösta stretched out her hand and caught it. It made me think of the video. That it used to snow here was hard to imagine.

"I have to tell you something, Gösta."

"Did you do something wrong?"

I looked around uneasily.

Gösta dropped the blossom. "Go on, spit it out."

"In the forest –" I didn't dare look up from the ground. "I found a child."

"A child? What are you talking about?"

"It's not from here. It's got bright red hair."

"How did a child make it into our territory?"

I shrugged.

"And now?"

"I brought it home."

"You know what the others will make of that."

"It's only a child."

"One that managed to get over our border. They won't accept that so easily. Maybe they'll declare it a changeling."

"A what?"

"You know the stories."

"You mean the fairy tales."

Gösta gave me a sharp look.

"Meisis isn't a changeling," I said.

"It's already got a name has it? Listen, girl, you must get rid of this child. Otherwise, you'll be held accountable." Gösta wanted to continue talking, but Len had opened the shutters in the house, leant over the sill, and called to us.

"We'll be right there," Gösta answered, and she said to me: "Make the child disappear tonight. Do it like my mother did. She drowned stray cats in the rain barrel. You just need a bag, rocks, and water that's deep enough. Believe me, you'd be doing the child a favour."

She got up from the bench. I followed her into the house with my eyes lowered. Len was standing in the corridor, where Gösta's butterfly collection was mounted in square glass display cases. The iridescent colours had faded long ago.

"Here," Len said, passing me a cloth bag filled with onions and eggs. "And I can offer you a bowlful of soup, I made too much yesterday."

I felt Gösta's hand on my back.

"I've got to do the mulching today," I said quickly.

My face was reflected in Len's sunglasses. For the first time, I was glad that she couldn't see me.

She laughed. "You're always so efficient."

Gösta pushed me through the door. I hugged the bag to my chest.

"Come back soon, you know I can always use some help," she said.

I nodded and stepped squinting into the gleaming sunlight. The door closed behind me.

EVERY PERSON COULD WEAR A MASK. BUT IT WOULD ALWAYS BE THE SAME FACE, CONCEALING THE FACT THAT THINGS HAVE CHANGED.

22.

Gösta told me the story of the territory. Before the bridge was blown up, she had worked as a hunter. Nobody knew their way around here as well as she did. Maybe that's also why Gösta was one of the first to notice things shifting.

"There were a few sunny days during my childhood, but it's always been cold here. Most of the time it was foggy. None of the houses had curtains, and cars would have to drive with their headlights on during the day. We were settled in this life, we had houses and farms. We were already fending for ourselves back then."

"And then… the animals. Birds, sometimes deer and wild boar. They were sick, straying our way. We knew they had come from the sea, and decided to blow up the concrete bridge, shutting off the only way in to completely shield us from whatever still might come. After blowing up the bridge, we had some good years. Everything that we needed we already had here, and nobody bothered us anymore. We could live how we had always wanted to. Only then the weather started to turn. Had you already been born at this point?"

I nodded.

"Then you most probably remember."

"Can you tell me anyway? What was it like for you both?"

Gösta sighed. "It was bad, terrible. First there were a few days with not a cloud in the sky. Then weeks, months. The fog became less dense. It frayed and only hung in the meadows early in the mornings and in the evenings. The bushes and trees were strange too. Even though it didn't rain they often came into bloom, but no longer bore fruit. The whole landscape began to shimmer in the heat. There were more and more insects. Our own animals died. We didn't know why.

We burned the dead cows, pigs, and horses in an open field. Mercifully, our chickens survived. It's madness, the landscape we had salvaged was betraying us. But we were in denial back then of course. We had to adapt, nonetheless. We stocked up, pumped fuel from the petrol stations, equipped ourselves with fly swatters, hung shimmery, yellow adhesive strips from our lamps where insects gradually perished, perfectly displayed in death. From the ever-blooming elderflower we made cordial. By the litre. Soon all the houses had an almost endless supply of it. We only drank water sweetened.

We had finally settled, as far as possible, into the new state of things. We were fortunate. The soil still yielded a modest harvest. The rabbits and hens survived the great death of the animals. We can adjust to the heat as well. We're frugal, that's how we're able to lead a simple life."

23.

On my way back I drove over the last remaining cobbled road. The vibrations made by the bumpy floor could be felt right up to the seat. I had rolled down the window and was smoking with my left hand, the right on the wheel. I saw Wolf and Levke sitting in the shade of the derelict bus stop from a long way off. They noticed me back and stood out in the middle of the road. I had to slow down and came to a stop right in front of them.

Their faces were sunburnt. They were wearing dark red sports jerseys, cutoff jeans and trainers. They each had a plastic bottle clamped under their arm that was filled with a brownish liquid. I could smell the homemade schnapps from the car.

People in the territory considered it a stroke of luck that the quince trees didn't suffer in the heat. The harvest was still so good that there were enough for the production of schnapps, which they had always distilled here.

Wolf and Levke grinned at me.

"What do you want?" I shouted over the running motor.

Levke leaned against the hood.

"Got any more?"

She pointed at the cigarette I was holding in my hand. Wolf ambled over to the driver's door and leant against the side mirror.

"We're itching for one" He mimed smoking while grabbing his crotch. His eyes were glazed over.

"As if you would have something that you could give me for it," I said.

Levke scratched the paint of the car with her nails. "Do you think you can just do anything you like?"

"Those who have nothing, get nothing. You taught me that."

"But we're not hiding a child at our house."

I looked her straight in the eyes.

"Had one too many again?" I asked.

Levke took a large, brazen gulp from the bottle and walked over to the other window.

"That a child with hair as red as anything stands around in your front garden, well, I couldn't make that up after ten bottles."

"I can vouch for that" shouted Wolf, "no one could think up a colour like that."

Levke spat on the passenger seat. She rubbed at it with the base of the bottle. "A little memento," she said. Wolf laughed mid-guzzle. I stubbed out the cigarette on the dashboard

"I really don't have time for your little games," I said.

"Now, don't be like that." Levke said, but gave Wolf a sign with the nod of her head and they stepped back from the car.

"You can't prove anything," I said.

"You better watch out," Levke said, taking another swig. "Don't forgot why the bridge got blown up."

"Fuck you!"

I hit the accelerator pedal, shifting into second gear.

In the rearview mirror I saw them once more standing in the middle of the road, holding their bottles in the air.

ON THE RUN IN A CLEARLY DELIMITED TERRITORY YOU START GOING IN CIRCLES. THE DISTANCE WILL NOT INCREASE, IT REMAINS TO MEASURE THE REAL DISTANCE IN YOUR MIND.

24.

I turned onto the sand track and rolled the pick-up up to the front of our house. My body felt numb with tension. Hunched over the steering wheel, I looked around through the windscreen, but nothing indicated that someone had been here.

In the hallway I heard a distant hissing sound coming from the living room. I slowly moved towards it.

Edith was lying on the carpet with the dogs next to the sofa. She was wearing a night-blue woollen dress with rolled-up sleeves. She had drawn her knees up to her chest and pillowed her head on her rabbit fur coat. Pressed against her ear she held the radio, which was usually always on the sideboard in the kitchen. She was turning the adjuster, it crackled loudly, and I heard the hissing sound again.

"What are you doing?," I asked, standing over her.

Edith rolled her eyes and told me she wanted to hear music.

"But the thing doesn't work properly," she added, "that's why it sounds a bit like the sea."

I would have liked to have punched her in the face. "The reception's been faulty for years," I said.

"But I sometimes still find a transmitter."

I became impatient. "What are you talking about?"

She held the radio stubbornly to her other ear. "You know, last night I dreamt of the sea. The churning water, and the way it threw itself again the dark rocks over and over again and how the salt stayed behind on the pebbles. Then waking up felt like I was sinking."

"Why are you telling me this?"

"Because it's the child's fault. It's bringing up the old images."

"Meisis?"

"Don't you feel like something's shifted since she's been in the house? The way she looks at me makes me nervous."

"You haven't moved from the sofa. When would you have seen her?"

"At night sometimes."

"I think you have sunstroke."

"Ask her," Edith said, grabbing a potato that was laying on the sofa. Dirt clung to the skin. She took a bite out of it.

"How many times have I told you that you can't eat them."

"I was hungry." She wiped her mouth.

"They have to be cooked, otherwise they're bad for your stomach," I said, taking the potato out of her hand.

"They taste better this way."

She tried to grab the potato, gripping my leg with her other hand, but I kicked her away, went to the window, opened it, and threw the potato into the front garden.

"Are you crazy?"

She crawled across the floor, knocking over one of the glasses while doing so. Water gushed over the carpet. I imagined kicking her head, and cracked my knuckles.

"Skalde?"

Meisis was standing in the doorway, holding a rabbit in her arms.

"Didn't I tell you to stay in the attic?"

Meisis shrugged her shoulders.

"It was so hot up there."

I turned away and tried to breath calmly.

"What's wrong?" Meisis asked, standing close to me.

"If I tell you to stay in the attic, you must do it, understand? No matter how long it lasts, and no matter how hot it gets."

Meisis nodded, the rabbit now tightly pressed to her chest.

Edith laughed. "Sounds familiar."

I ignored her.

"What's wrong with the rabbit?"

"It's not moving anymore," she said.

"Show me."

She hesitated and threw a look at Edith.

"Give it to me now."

I grabbed the rabbit and examined it. The eyes were gummy with pus. It wasn't breathing.

"What did you do to it?" I asked.

"Nothing, it was already like that when I took it out of the hutch."

"It's dead," I said, "now all we can do is eat it."

Meisis nodded.

I walked off and took the rabbit into the kitchen.

Later, I threw another look into the living room. Edith hadn't moved. I closed the door and went to Meisis in the kitchen, where I wiped the blood from the wax table cloth and began to roast the rabbit.

IT SEEMS TO ME AS IF THE WALLS OF THE HOUSE ARE MADE OF PAPER, THE WALLS ARE MUCH TOO DELICATE, AS IF IT COULD BE FOLDED TOGETHER, BURNED DOWN, REDUCED TO ASHES IN JUST A FEW SIMPLE STEPS.

25.

The sun stood crimson over the pine forest. In its light, the garden appeared as if lacquered. The child was still sleeping. Edith had been lying in the bathtub since yesterday evening. I stood in the kitchen and could hear her moving in the water above me.

I took the butchering knife from the dresser. I washed it thoroughly, readied the grindstone and began sharpening it. The even motion soothed me.

I concentrated on the task until I could make out the soft sound of an approaching car. Tires scrunched in the sand, the engine fell silent. I put the grindstone to one side, grabbed the knife and crept to the front door. I held the knife so tightly, my fingernails bore into my palm. There was a knock.

"Anybody there?"

More knocking. I hid the knife behind me in my belt and opened the door a crack. On the lower steps stood Pesolt. He ran his hand through his blond, shoulder-length hair and wiped his hands on his stained tracksuit. I looked past him at his car. The number plate was missing. The headlights were smashed. There was a deep dent in the passenger side door. But the seat was empty.

"What do you want?" I asked.

"Someone moved in?"

"Who says?"

"Wolf and Levke saw a child standing in your front garden."

I acted surprised. "A child?"

I could see from Pesolt's face that he didn't buy it.

"You believe something those wasters told you?"

He climbed a step higher. "Then let me in."

"And if I don't?"

"It wasn't a question."

I felt a draft of air behind me. I turned around. Edith was standing in the dark hallway. She was only wearing her rabbit fur coat. Her wet hair dripped onto the flagstones.

"You will leave my plot right now," she said, standing next to me.

Pesolt grinned. "You mean Nuuel's plot?"

Edith raised her chin. "Do we really want to talk about our dead?"

For a moment I thought he was going to lose his cool, but his features relaxed.

"You're really not making this easy," he said, turning around.

He slowly went back to his car. He opened the door, but turned towards us one more time.

"Everyone can't just do whatever they want around here," he said, as if it was a good thing.

I bit my lip.

"We know that," Edith replied.

Pesolt nodded and got into his car. He revved the engine, accelerated and turned onto the road.

Edith pushed me into the house, closed the door and turned the key. I was about to say something, but she shook her head and went upstairs without saying another word.

I kept Meisis in the house all day. We closed all the curtains and went up to the attic. I lay down on the floorboards, exhausted, and watched her while she slid the snail shells she'd found in the garden back and forth across the wood. There were hardly any living ones left. Only the empty houses remained.

"Am I going to have to leave?" Meisis asked, picking up

the smallest snail shell and holding it in the narrow shaft of sunlight falling in through the curtains.

"What makes you think that?"

"You didn't tell the man outside the truth," she said.

"You could hear us?"

"Will he come back?" Meisis asked, putting the snail shell with the others.

"Maybe."

"And then?"

I rolled onto my back and stared at the ceiling. "We'll cross that bridge when we come to it."

26.

My sleep was so light that I kept waking with a start. The forest stood darkly outside. No moon in sight.

I could hear Edith walking below through the house and a couple of times I had the feeling she was standing directly beneath the hatch leading to the attic.

At daybreak, I couldn't take it anymore. I got up, got dressed and went downstairs. The tiredness made me fuzzy. I came across Edith in the hallway.

"Didn't you sleep?" she asked me, burying her hands in the pockets of her coat.

"Barely," I replied.

Once in the kitchen, I made coffee. I hadn't touched the tin in years. I had wanted to save it for a moment when I would really need it. I poured some in a cup for myself, filled a second, and set it in front of Edith, who had sat down at the table.

"You should never have taken in the child," she said.

I said nothing.

"Do you realise what you've started?"

"If I hadn't have taken her in, who would have?"

"They would have made it disappear. We wouldn't have known anything about it," Edith said.

"You see."

"Yes, but now we're in danger too."

"Nuuel took you in."

At the name of my father, Edith winced.

"There was resistance then too, but he wasn't afraid."

"Of course he was afraid."

"If he was still alive, he would have taken in Meisis."

Edith was silent.

"Don't you believe it could be different this time? Everyone's tired."

"In this regard they will never change."

"What makes you so sure of it?"

"You didn't experience what it was like. They would have rather let their apples rot on the compost than give me one."

"That's over twenty years ago."

"You heard Pesolt yesterday."

I took a sip from my cup.

"Right now, we're being closely monitored," she said.

"I won't send the child away."

"Then you have to be ready to live with the consequences.

When I think back on that conversation in the kitchen, it seems as if it was the first time we had spoken to each other normally in years. We didn't accuse one another of anything, just discussed the facts. We weren't in agreement, and yet we hadn't argued.

HOW LONG CAN I STAND UPRIGHT, HOLD UP MY OWN BODY THAT FORCES ME TO MY KNEES TWICE AS HARD.

27.

The dogs were restless that morning already. Time and time again they would get up, trot aimlessly through the house, lie down in other places, twitch in their sleep and jump up at the slightest sound. They must have had a premonition.

People neared the house from the back, came from the forest and stood at the border of our plot, in the middle of the day. Two women, three men. I didn't know all their names; their farms were further away. But I knew that they all had a lot of land, I could tell from their bulky gold rings set with amber and wild boar teeth. Their clothes made from bright linen. Pesolt was also among them. He stayed in the background for the moment.

The child was crouching near the pool in the shade of a sheet I'd stretched between two trees. When she noticed the group, she hid the building blocks in the grass.

"So it's true," said one of the women. She had a severe face. It didn't fit with her graceful body. She nodded to the others, and they came closer. I put myself between them and Meisis.

"Liar," Pesolt said to me.

"How did you get into the territory?" the woman asked, but Meisis didn't respond.

She turned to me impatiently. "Does it understand?"

I nodded.

She repeated her question.

Meisis's face remained expressionless.

"Kindly answer us," the woman said, indicating to me with a movement of her head that I should step aside. I stayed where I was.

"It's only a child," I said, "what are you all afraid of?"

"It's not wanted here," the woman with the stern face said, "It won't bother any of you, you won't even notice it's here."

"That's not the point. It doesn't belong here. The hair alone..." The man pointed to Meisis, as if she were an animal.

"But where's she meant to go?" I asked, grabbing Meisis' hand. She leant against me sleepily.

"Back where it came from," Pesolt said.

A vehicle sounded its horn. I spun around. A Jeep came to a stop next to the house. The door burst open, and Gösta climbed out. She came striding towards us in mud-smeared rubber boots.

"What's all this?" she asked, standing next to me.

"They've taken in a child that's not from here," the man said.

Pesolt cleared his throat. "It won't tell us where it came from."

Gösta grasped her long grey hair, twisted it into a knot and pinned it up. In that moment, her gaunt body lost all of its fragility. She looked like a robust piece of wood.

"Since when have you been afraid of a child?" she asked.

"But its hair," the woman protested.

'She looks like a changeling," the man concurred.

Gösta laughed. "Aren't we all a bit too old for this?"

"We can't make any exceptions," Pesolt said.

"I will vouch for this child," Gösta said. "Nothing will happen. And if it does, I'll see that it disappears. And Skalde along with it," she pointed to me.

"You must swear it," the woman said, "on Len and on the territory."

Gösta nodded and raised her hand. Pesolt bit his lip.

"Was that everything?" Gösta dropped her hand. "Then we can bring this meeting to an end."

For a moment no one moved. They only relaxed when Pesolt gave them the sign and they fought their way back into the forest.

Gösta turned to me. The tiredness was once more written on her face. I put out my arm so she could support herself against me, but instead she spat on the ground at my feet.

"I can do it myself," she snapped at me and hobbled back to her car. Meisis and I followed her. At the car door Gösta said:

"You can thank Len. If it was up to me, I would have just handed over the child. I won't help you a second time, understand? I want my peace."

"I know," I said quickly.

She nodded and threw a glance at Meisis.

"That's what you're risking everything for?" Shaking her head, she climbed into the Jeep.

As she drove off, Meisis took my hand.

"Why are they scared of me?" she asked.

"Because you're not like them," I replied.

I DREAMT OF INVISIBLE DOGS WHOSE BARKS FADED AWAY IN THE FOREST. MY HANDS WERE BALLED INTO FISTS, BUT I KNEW THAT I COULDN'T OPEN THEM BECAUSE BETWEEN MY FINGERS I HELD FLUTTERING INSECTS THAT WANTED TO FLY AWAY.

28.

Kurt and I had been sitting at the edge of the pool, I was smoking my first cigarette when he told me the story of my parents. Perhaps he sensed that Edith concealed everything from me.

Edith first arrived in the territory after the concrete bridge was blown up. She was suddenly standing in the fog in broad daylight in the middle of the road that led to the river. Her rose-coloured silk dress was completely wet through. A swimsuit shimmered through the fabric. She had a silver roller suitcase with her.

To the question of how she had made it across the river, she refused to answer, even though Pesolt and Gösta interrogated her the whole night long.

Her suitcase was filled with more clothes and her mother-of-pearl jewellery. Aside from that she had five lipsticks in different shades of red and a brush with a handle made of driftwood.

They told her that she wasn't allowed to stay in the territory, there was no place for her here.

"How can I go back when the place I came from no longer exists?", Edith asked with an expressionless face, but nobody cared.

They gave her three days, then she would have to leave the territory again.

For two whole days Edith walked around aimlessly and spent the nights beneath the humming electricity pylons.

On the third day Edith found the pool in Nuuel's garden, knocked on his door, and he let her in the house as if they had known each other for years.

It soon got out where Edith was hiding. People came to Nuuel's house and told Edith to show herself, but Nuuel didn't open up. They decided to come back the next day. If necessary, they would gain entry by force.

That night, the dogs disappeared from the farms. They reappeared on Nuuel's plot and guarded the house. They obeyed Edith and ate from her hand. No one came.

Nuuel asked people to tolerate Edith. She was only one woman, what were they afraid of? He promised them that they would get their dogs back. After the others had conferred for a long time, they finally yielded.

"As long as she blends in and behaves discreetly, we will allow for her to live in your house."

Edith released the dogs, and the people left the plot. They avoided Nuuel's house from then on and stopped greeting them.

The accident happened a year later.

Nuuel often went along the river to skim stones. What he was doing there that day, when hardly anything could be seen through the fog, no one could explain.

They found him that evening floating face down in the water. Of course, it was Edith who was made responsible for his death. They showed up at the house with his bloated corpse, lay Nuuel's drowned body on the doormat and knocked.

They didn't know that Edith was pregnant. They only saw when she opened the door. Their plan to shoot her on the spot was abandoned. They still had a scrap of humanity after all.

They left Edith the dead body and drove off. She had to dig the grave all by herself. At dawn, Kurt came and brought her a lilac bush, they planted it beside it.

"And then?" I asked Kurt, running the back of my hand over my dry lips.

"And then? And then nothing. She stayed here in the house."

Kurt put out his cigarette and flicked it into the pool, "And then you were born."

YOUR MOTHER CAME OUT OF THE WATER, DO YOU SLEEP IN A PUDDLE TOO? THE OTHER CHILDREN ASK ME, LAUGHING ALL THE WHILE.

29.

"Was someone here?" Edith wanted to know that evening. She had just come out of the bath and met me on the landing. Her feet left wet imprints on the floor. She stood before me somewhat lost and pinched her face where her skin had started to peel. She pulled off a loose flake and rolled it between her fingers into a little ball.

"Pesolt came with a couple of others. They know now that the child lives here," I said.

Edith didn't say anything.

"They wanted for it to go," I added.

"You're not really surprised, are you?"

I shrugged.

"And now?" she asked,

"Gösta came and convinced them to hold off."

Edith's body stiffened. She lowered her hand. "Gösta was there too?"

"She came later."

"Naturally. The noble Gösta. Helped you out again has she?"

I screwed up my eyes. "Yes, she did. There was no one else there."

"You do know that in the end it won't make any difference? Even Gösta can't change that the child isn't from here. Sooner or later, they will find a reason for why it has to leave."

I stood close to Edith.

"If none of it matters, why didn't you just give the child to Pesolt, when you had the chance?"

Edith didn't reply straight away. "You know I can still do that." Her gaze was cold.

"You wouldn't."

She grinned. "Don't you believe me?"

I moved back. Edith now stood as straight as a pole and looked anything but lost. "If you want to put your life in jeopardy, then go ahead, but keep me out of it," she said.

"But you have no life. Look at yourself. You haven't left the plot for years. Do you want to just keep going? Do you call this having a life?"

Edith's face remained unmoving. "The only thing I'm asking is that you don't get me mixed up in it, is that understood?"

"You've made yourself very clear. I've never been able to rely on you for help," my voice cracked, and I had to turn away.

"Go on, cry, I'm sure Gösta will be on her way to comfort you."

Edith said something else, but I didn't hear it as I'd climbed up into the attic and slammed the hatch down after me.

30.

I stood with Meisis behind the shed showing her how to cut the stinging nettles without injuring herself, when Edith stepped out the backdoor. She had brushed her hair up into two thick plaits, put on dark lipstick and was wearing a blue silk dress under her rabbit fur coat. She approached us with purpose.

"What do you want?" I asked, as she appeared in front of us.

"I thought you both might need a little help."

"In this get up?"

Edith raised her chin. "Have you forgotten how I used to look when I made mulch? As if I couldn't do it in a fur coat."

"But you need gloves," Meisis said.

Edith smiled. "Is there a pair left?"

Meisis nodded. "Skalde got mine from the dresser in the hall. There were more I think."

"Would you go and get them for me?"

"Sure." Meisis pressed the knife into my hand and went into the house.

Without looking at Edith, I asked: "What are you up to?"

"My God, do I have to justify offering my help?"

"Yesterday you were talking about handing Meisis over to Pesolt, and today you suddenly want to help us in the garden, when you haven't lifted a finger in years?"

My voice was louder than I had intended.

Edith buried her hands in the pockets of the fur coat. "I'm anxious about our safety. I didn't mean it like that."

"What did you mean then?"

"Don't keep going on about it, I just don't want you to

think that because Gösta put in a good word for you that you don't have to worry anymore."

I took off my gloves and wiped the sweat from my face. "What do you mean by that?"

"With the child. The situation. You have to have a plan."

"Gösta vouched for her. Nothing will happen. And with time people will get used to Meisis. In a couple of years, they won't know anymore that she's not one of them."

Edith laughed. "They never got used to me, and I've been here for twenty-five years."

"But that's your own fault."

Edith didn't say anything, then she said: "And how do you propose to do it? Are you going to drag her to all of the farms and introduce her to everyone or something?"

"What's wrong with that?" I asked. "Better than locking her in the house and acting like she doesn't exist."

"Do you really think they'll be convinced that easily? Have you learned nothing in all these years?"

"They're not bad people," I said.

"They are, but you never wanted to believe me."

"You want to give me advice? You? Who do you think you are?"

Edith flinched. As if I had slapped her in the face. She almost stumbled.

"Then give it a try," she said, wiping her mouth, smearing the lipstick, trying to smile.

"That's what I'm planning to do," I said, putting the gloves back on, grabbing the stinging nettles and carrying them into the shed.

When I came back, Edith was gone. Meisis returned with another pair of gloves. She looked around searchingly.

"She changed her mind," I said.

Disappointed, Meisis lay the gloves on the ground. I passed her the knife. "We'll do it alone."

While we were cutting the rest of the stinging nettles, we were silent. Meisis lifted her head and looked at the house many times, but Edith didn't reappear.

It didn't occur to me at the time that Edith wanted to get along with me in the garden. That she regretted what she had said the day before, that she was trying to climb over the rifts between us that had become deeper and deeper over the years.

THERE ARE DAYS I WISH THAT THE BODY OF MY MOTHER WAS LYING BURIED BENEATH THE WEEDS.

31.

Edith was gone for three days. Only her sheet lay on the sofa in the living room. I looked in the bathroom, but that was empty too. She'd even drained the water from the tub. It was as if she had evaporated into thin air, and I believed that my long-held wish had been fulfilled.

Meisis was aware of Edith's absence too. She didn't ask after her, but she spent a remarkable amount of time on the lower floor, where she kept building new towers out of Edith's books. It wasn't until the fourth night that I found out where Edith was hiding. I walked past her room and saw that, under her wardrobe doors, light was coming through.

She stayed there a whole week.

TO NEVER LEAVE A WARDROBE AGAIN.
TWO SQUARE METRES OF LIVING SPACE WITH
DAYLIGHT LOCKED OUT, WHO WOULD MISS YOU?

32.

When I came into the kitchen, Edith was standing motionless in the darkness.

"Don't you want to turn on the light?" I asked.

Edith didn't react. I went and stood next to her.

In the twilight I saw multiple figures with dogs walking across the meadow and disappearing into the forest. There was more barking coming from off in the distance.

"A search party," Edith said. "There was another group before. All going in the direction of the river."

"Why?" I asked.

"Isn't it obvious? They want to find out how a child managed to make it into the territory," Edith said.

I was surprised by the harshness in her voice. "And if they find something?"

"It would be for the best."

We stared silently out the window. It had become so dark that we could only make out their silhouettes.

"I saw them moving exactly like this before they brought me Nuuel's body. I happened to be standing at the window and I watched it. I didn't think anything of it," Edith said.

There was a pause. I held my breath and hoped that she would keep talking.

"What are you doing?" asked Meisis. I flew around, startled. She was standing in the brightly lit rectangle of the door. Her face lay in darkness.

"You should have been asleep ages ago?" I walked over to her. She didn't move. It was only when I held out my hand to her that she stepped towards me.

"I heard your voices. And dogs barking outside."

"Nothing's happened that you should be scared of," I said.

Edith laughed. "I wouldn't put it like that."

I didn't go into it. "Come on, I'll take you to bed."

"Will you stay until I fall asleep?"

I nodded, lifted her up, and carried her upstairs to her room.

Once there I lay her on the sofa bed and covered her.

"Too warm," she said and ran her hand over her face.

"I can open the window, but it won't make any difference."

"Still," Meisis said, reaching her hand out towards me. "Why are they going into the forest?" she wanted to know.

She noticed my hesitation and sat up.

"You have to tell me."

"They're trying to find out which route you took to reach the territory."

"That's why they're going into the forest?"

"They're heading towards the river."

"So they're starting their search at the river?"

I nodded.

My answer seemed to relieve Meisis. I dozed off, but the dogs were still barking in my dreams.

33.

I wanted to prove to Edith that she was wrong and resolved to take the child with me to Eggert. I thought that Eggert would be a good place to start.

I parked the pick-up in front of his yard on the stone slab path, and Meisis and I climbed out. We walked through the gate together.

Eggert was standing by the lush border of flowers he had planted around the lime trees in the middle of the triangular yard he stubbornly maintained. The heat intensified the heavy scent of the blossoms.

I looked around for the sheepdogs that usually patrolled the farm, but I couldn't see them anywhere, their chains lay loose in the gravel.

Eggert was crouched over pulling dried up stalks from the shrubbery and throwing them in the wheelbarrow. When he saw us coming over, he stopped moving.

"That child needs to leave my yard right now," he said.

"That child is called Meisis," I said.

"I couldn't care less what its name is. Pesolt told us all about it. She can't just walk around in my yard like that in any case."

I bent over to Meisis and told her to go back to the car and wait for me there. "It won't take long," I whispered.

With her head bowed, Meisis walked back to the pick-up. I could see her disappointment.

I walked back over to Eggert.

"Does she look like she could be of any danger?" I asked.

"The hair seems very ominous to me."

"You'll all get used to it sooner or later."

"She doesn't belong here."

I didn't push it any further, pointed to the pick-up's truck bed and said: "I've brought you the two canisters I promised you."

Eggert looked at me blankly, his forehead rumpled

"The mulch for your flowers and the garden, I was supposed to bring them over today."

"I said that before you found the child."

"Gösta vouched for Meisis."

Eggert took a handkerchief from his trousers and wiped the sweat from his bald head. "Oh yes, Gösta." He stuffed the handkerchief back into his pocket.

"Listen, Skalde, you've brought all this on yourself. Imagine if all of us just did whatever we felt like doing without thinking even for a second how it would affect the others, what consequences it would bring. Here in the territory, we follow each other's lead. This is why things are going relatively well for us. Here, we don't think of ourselves first, we think of the community, of the territory. Your mother's never wanted to understand that either."

"Even though it's nothing more than a child or –"

Eggert raised his hand. "It's not about that," he said.

I swallowed.

"I'll take your canisters, but as soon as there's even the smallest nonsense here you can forget all about me trading anything with you." He threw down his gloves onto the wheelbarrow. "Come inside and bring the mulch with you."

I nodded. On the way to the pick-up I tried to kick a stone, but I just missed it. Meisis rolled down the window and leaned out towards me.

"I can help you; I can carry one, too," she said. I shook my head.

"Stay in the car."

I took the canisters from the truck bed and followed Eggert into the house. Piled up in the entrance way were trainers belonging to Eggert's daughters.

"Put them down anywhere, I'll be right back," Eggert said, disappearing into the hallway.

I was in the process of sliding the cannisters under the stairs, when Levaii, Eggert's youngest daughter, came downstairs. She leant over the rail and eyed me up. Her irises were so pale that I was scared by her gaze.

"What are you doing here?" she asked suspiciously.

"I brought over some mulch"

Without letting me out of her sight, Levaii unravelled the end of her braid and dropped it onto her shoulder.,

"Where are your sisters?" I asked.

"Outside for sure, they're digging in the garden." Levaii said.

She was still staring at me. She didn't blink once.

"This child that's living with you –," she faltered.

"Yes?" I asked, folding my arms across my chest.

"Aren't you a bit scared of it?"

"What do you mean?"

"Oh, you know, don't you think it's a bit weird that it suddenly showed up even though it's been so closed off here for so many years? And then there's its hair," she paused meaningfully. "Well, I'd be scared if it was sleeping in the same house as me."

I was glad Eggert came back into the kitchen.

When he saw Levaii he snapped at her: "What are you still doing inside? Your sisters have been working in the garden for two hours already. Go on, get out there."

"I'm going, I'm going," she reluctantly took the last few

steps, nodded at me and left the house. She left the door open. In the bright sunlight that fell in, I noticed for the first time how filthy the room was. Even the trainers were covered in a fine layer of dust.

"I'm really hoping that it's just a phase," Eggert said, looking after his youngest daughter.

"I'm sure it is," I said.

He turned to me and handed me five jars of preserved fruit. "Had to look around a bit, they were right at the back of the cupboard."

"Thank you."

"You better go," he said, rushing me back out.

While reversing the pick-up I saw Levaii and her sisters behind the house in the dirt of the vegetable patch. The pieces of cloth they tied around their heads as protection from the sun stood out brightly from their surroundings. They worked the dry earth with spades and hoes. The sweat shone on their muscular arms.

Levaii looked furious, but her sisters smiled at us. One of them even raised a hand in farewell.

I hit the accelerator and we drove away.

The plots that we passed were empty of people. It seemed as if they had all withdrawn into the interiors of their houses. Sometimes I thought I could see someone standing behind the bright curtains, but we were going so fast I was never quite sure.

"Can we just keep going please?" Meisis asked, closing her eyes.

"We can't. At some point we can't go any further."

Why not?"

"There's a river."
"But isn't there a bridge?"
I shook my head.
"But couldn't we just go in the other direction?"
"That's dead territory. We'd die there."

34.

Pesolt's house lay in a dip. In this part of the territory there was no asphalt road, only a gravel path. I parked the pick-up up on the overhang, took out the bag with the rabbit in it and got out with Meisis. Voices carried over to us, but I couldn't locate them. They didn't seem to be coming from a specific direction, and there was no one in view either.

"Stay close to me," I instructed Meisis. We walked next to each other over the gravel towards the house.

To the left and right the hollyhocks bloomed a dark purple, almost black. We climbed up the steps to the front door, and I knocked. Nothing happened. I knocked again, but no one opened up.

"Maybe someone's out back in the garden," I said, taking Meisis's hand and going with her once around the house. The lawn, scorched by the sun, was cut so short that the earth was visible below it. The flower beds were shrouded with a bright material. The meadow orchard started immediately behind them. The squat trees barely made a shadow. I saw that there were not yet ripe apples hanging from some of them. A fence marked the perimeter. There stood Pesolt, painting the wooden slats red. The fresh colour glowed unnaturally in the landscape. We approached him hesitantly. When he saw us coming, he lay down his paintbrush on the can and wiped his paint-smeared fingers down his trousers.

"Don't remember giving an invitation last time we saw one another," he said grimly.

"A couple of weeks ago you said you'd come take a look at our fruit trees."

Pesolt laughed. "Did I?"

"Yes," I looked at him defiantly. "I told you that they only bloom and that the last harvest was a year ago."

"You're not the only ones." Pesolt rubbed his brow.

"When we talked about it, you promised me – "

"That was before you took in the child."

"Your mother planted those trees," I said. "A cherry tree and a plum tree."

No one knew how to deal with fruit trees as well as Pesolt. His mother taught him everything. And she in turn had learned it from her father. Pesolt's trees still always produced a reasonable yield. How he did it, he had so far revealed to no one.

"I've brought you half a rabbit," I said, and held the plastic bag out towards him.

He threw a glance at Meisis. "Is that all?"

"And a canister of mulch," I said, "it's still on the truck bed in the pick-up."

"What do I need fertiliser for? I'm not growing anything else, and I don't need it for my fruit trees, they bear fruit no matter what."

"What do you want then?"

He hesitated before saying. "Edith's got that knife. The handle's made of pinewood."

I knew straightaway what he was talking about. A handy knife, the blade no longer than my index finger. Edith always kept it close to her. When she went to sleep, she shoved it between the cushions of the sofa.

Once she forgot it on the table, and I used it to peel potatoes. When Edith came back into the kitchen and saw me with the knife, she took it away from me so abruptly the blade left a deep cut in the palm of my hand.

I said to Pesolt: "Not that, that belongs to Edith."

"Yeah, and? Is she not in need of a good fruit yield?"

Meisis was getting restless, I put my hand on her shoulder. "There must be something else I could give you," I said.

Pesolt shook his head. "I want the knife."

Something hardened in my stomach. "You'll get three rabbits. Three strong ones."

"I want the knife," Pesolt said, picking up the brush and continuing to paint the worn slats. I bit my tongue so hard I tasted blood.

"We're going," I said to Meisis.

Pesolt straightened up. "When you change your mind, you know where to find me."

He wanted to touch my shoulder, but I took a step back and pulled Meisis with me. Pesolt laughed.

Pesolt's twins were sitting on the steps leading to the front door of the house. Meisis stood there as if rooted to the ground. The twins started squealing and rushed over to us.

"Hey," they said, stationing themselves in front of us, their arms at their sides, their stomachs pushed out. They were wearing the same pyjamas. The pattern was made of apples and pears, the trouser legs and sleeves were too short for them, and on their knees the fabric was crusted with blood, as if they had already fallen countless times on the gravel track.

"Leave us alone" I said.

"We're not doing anything," they replied, simultaneously prodding each other in the side with their elbows.

"Why didn't you give our father the knife?"

"He doesn't need a knife," I said.

"How do you know that?"

I didn't respond and wanted to keep moving, but they stood in our way.

"You won't have anything else to eat soon if your trees totally wither away."

"We have potatoes and rabbits," I said.

The twins laughed. "Our father said that only people with fruit trees will survive."

"How does he know that?" Meisis asked.

"Our father has always known things before the others knew them."

Meisis shrugged her shoulders. I quickly said: "We won't go hungry," and pushed passed them with Meisis. We took big strides up the hill to the pick-up.

By the time I had turned the car around, the twins had disappeared back into the house. The white curtains billowed in the breeze. Len once told me that the people here always used to leave a window open in spite of the cold weather, because according to superstition, unwanted strangers would stay away if the wind could get into the house.

35.

Back at the house, I hid Meisis in the attic.

"You will not move from this spot," I said. Meisis wanted to protest, but I shook my head and said: "I won't be long."

I didn't pay attention to which way I was going. It helped me that the distance between the house and me was becoming greater and greater. My head emptied out. When I heard a birdcall, I stopped. The birdcall came again. I followed it. The dry branches cracked beneath my feet. Sunlight fell between the straight trunks down to the ground. The quarry appeared before me in the forest. I thought that the bird was to be found there and approached slowly.

Between the scrapped cars at the bottom of the pit lay Wolf and Levke. Wolf was on his back and sleeping. Levke on the other hand had her eyes open. It was she who was imitating the birdcall. In the next moment she sprang up, came at me, brought me down and held me to the ground, breathing hard.

"Do you really think I hadn't noticed you coming ages ago?"

"I didn't mean to sneak up."

"Oh no?"

"I hadn't heard a bird in such a long time."

"It wasn't just any bird. It was a starling. You really don't know anything. You're always acting like you know stuff, but you can't even recognise a starling."

Levke could mimic all the birds that used to be in the territory. As a child she had often walked around outside for hours imitating different kinds of birds. The other children would follow her, loudly yelling, all the while hoping that a real bird would be lured out. I had always watched the procession from afar, until I had finally built up the courage to join them. I had to be the very last one in the queue, those were the rules, but at least they let me follow them.

To my surprise, Levke once really managed to trick a bird. It flapped over our group and seemed to respond to Levke's voice. One of the girls, who was walking closely behind Levke, drew out her slingshot, but Levke turned around, grabbed her by the collar and punched her multiple times in the face.

"You won't do that a second time," she said. The girl writhed on the ground; her hands pressed over her face. Blood dripped from her chin onto the sand. None of the others moved. Levke started walking again, and we followed her. We left the girl behind.

A week later the incident was forgotten. The girl carried on walking with the group, but they shouted at me until they'd frightened me away.

Levke got off of me and sat crossed legged next to Wolf, who was still sleeping.

She waved her hand at me. "Now, fuck off."

I got to my feet. "Is Wolf okay?"

"Drank too much. He'll sleep until it gets dark."

"And you?"

Levke twisted her mouth. "I can hold it more." She reached for her bottle, which had rolled under one of the cars, and took a swig. "Where'd you leave the child?"

"At the house."

"Are you locking it up now or something?"

"Just because I didn't bring it with me this once?"

Wolf murmured something in his sleep and turned onto

his stomach. He buried his bloated face in the crook of his arm. Levke picked her teeth.

"No one wants the child here, you know that. Why won't you see it?"

I didn't respond, then I said: "It's not doing anything to you."

"Up to now nothing good has happened when a stranger shows up here."

"You mean when Edith showed up here?"

"There are other stories. Even before the bridge was blown up."

"What kind of stories?"

"I heard my grandparents talking about it once. People came and alleged that the houses belonged to them. Showed them important looking papers. Didn't do them much good. They didn't get anyone out of course."

"What happened to them?"

"Man, no idea. Disappeared into thin air or just ended up in the river. Who knows?"

My stomach tightened.

"They had their reasons for blowing up the bridge," Levke said.

"Are you scared of the child?" I asked.

Levke got up and came right up to me. Her breath smelled strongly of alcohol. "We want everything to stay how it is, why don't you get that?"

"I want that too," I protested.

"Then start acting like it."

She shoved me out of the way. For a moment I was tempted to lunge at her and hit her in the face with both fists, but I knew I was no match for her in a fight. I glowered at her and took my time climbing back up the slope.

NO ONE GETS TO HAVE THE DARK.
YOUR DEBRIS STAYS IN YOUR HEAD.
WHAT IS TO BE DONE WITH A PAIN THAT CANNOT BE
DISPOSED OF?

36.

I reached the house, but something seemed different.

The dogs were lying in the hallway, they got up and followed me. The sofa in the living room was empty. Edith had left her coat on the cushions. I called for Meisis, but received no reply. The dogs followed me into the kitchen, their claws clicked on the tiles. I called for Meisis, again, yet I didn't hear a sound. I filled a glass with water from the jug. I took a sip, it tasted rusty. The dogs trotted to the window and whined. I looked outside.

In the garden beneath the cherry tree sat Edith and Meisis on a sheet in the shade.

I put the glass down and stepped outside through the front backdoor.

"What are you doing?" I asked. The dogs, who had followed me, lay down next to Edith on the sheet.

She reached out her hand and ran it through their coat. "Is it forbidden to sit in the garden?"

Meisis smiled at me. She was wearing a pair of Edith's silk pyjamas.

"Where's your t-shirt?" I asked.

"She can't wear the same thing every day," Edith said.

"That's why she's wearing your clothes?"

"She has to wear something."

Edith had shortened the sleeves and trouser legs.

Meisis showed me the leftover fabric. "Edith said I can have it."

"What do you want that for?"

Meisis lowered her eyes.

"I might have other things. I'll look later," said Edith.

I nodded, not showing any emotion.

"Do you want to sit with us?" Meisis asked, trying to shove one of the dogs over.

I shook my head and went back into the house without another word.

My body felt heavy. In slow motion I climbed up to the attic, opened the hatch and went over to the cardboard boxes holding my clothes. I laid them all out on the mattress and lay down.

37.

I MOVE THROUGH THE LAND IN CAMOUFLAGE, SO THAT NO ONE CAN FIND ME.

Even when I was still close to Edith, I was never allowed to wear her clothes. Instead, she sewed me basic trousers and tops from sheets and bedcovers. I wore them until they fell apart. If they became too short for me, Edith lengthened them with leftover fabric.

When the other children saw me for the first time, they laughed at me and called me scarecrow.

I asked Len and Gösta for clothes. They immediately understood, no questions asked, and brought me over a box. Inside I found two pairs of loose-fitting trousers, three button-downs, two t-shirts and a jumper. Everything in brown and beige tones. The t-shirts had been washed so many times that their printed slogans could no longer be deciphered. I tried on everything in front of Edith's wardrobe mirror and tried to walk like the other children in the territory, wide-legged, with a fearless stare.

Edith saw me for the first time in the new clothes the following day. She was standing with the dogs in the hallway as I came downstairs. The dogs growled and bared their teeth. Edith surveyed me from head to toe. I was wearing a shirt and jogging bottoms. I had unbranded trainers on. I knew that I looked like someone from the territory.

"Do you like it?" I asked, turning in a circle.

"I've never seen anything so ugly," she replied. My face remained expressionless.

I gathered together the things Edith had sewn for me and threw them in a pile in the garden. I was certain that Edith was watching through one of the windows, turned towards the house and set the clothes alight. When only smouldering embers remained, I went back inside.

Edith never found out that I sometimes secretly put on her clothes. I only did it when I was sure she was sleeping.

That Edith's clothes were so different to those worn by people in the territory fascinated me. I could spend hours putting them on and taking them off in front of the mirrored wardrobe in her room. While doing so I imagined that the house was different too, the landscape new, the sea no longer far away. I combed my hair with Edith's brush and read poetry about dunes. When I slipped back into my own things, I felt ashamed and each time swore to myself to never dress up again. But that never lasted long. I only stopped when I found clothes belonging to Nuuel. I was fifteen, maybe sixteen and tidying the basement. That was when I discovered a cavity behind a hatch, inside were multiple plastic bags.

I pulled them out and carried them to my room. It was only there that I dared to look inside them. Many pairs of trousers made from coarse material. Two thick woollen pullovers. Socks, underwear. A handful of t-shirts, undyed. I knew straight away that they had belonged to Nuuel.

They were clothes that other people in the territory wore.

I carefully pulled on one of the pairs of trousers and slipped on a top. The scent was familiar to me, but maybe I had just convinced myself that this was the case. I tried to imagine how my father had moved in them. He seemed not to have been much taller than I was. I only had to cuff the legs once.

When Edith saw me in them later, she looked at me in disbelief.

"Take those off right now," she said.

"I don't think Nuuel would mind his daughter wearing his clothes," I said.

Edith didn't respond and left me standing in the hallway.

She shut herself in the bathroom for weeks. I didn't see her at all.

38.

I was standing at the open window. People were walking across the meadows again. They moved through the heat almost in slow motion. They had dogs with them, but I couldn't hear any barking. A strange, impenetrable silence lay over the scenery. One by one they disappeared into the forest, only the last person paused and turned in my direction. Even though they were far away, I had the feeling they were looking at me. I didn't dare move. The person was still too. It seemed like an eternity in which neither of us moved. It was only when a garbled shout was heard that the person followed the others into the forest.

39.

Kurt was standing motionlessly in our garden, so close to the pool that, if he were to lose his balance, he would fall in. His rabbit fur coat shone wanly in the sunlight. He wasn't wearing shoes; his bare legs were scratched.

"What do you want?" I called while walking over to him.

"Levaii's sisters have gone missing," he said with a serious expression.

I stopped. "What do you mean they've gone missing?"

"They can't be found. As if swallowed up by the ground."

"Since when?"

"Eggert had noticed they were missing yesterday morning. He waited until midday, then he sent Levaii to tell the others. Now they're all looking, but there's still not been a trace. I wanted to warn you."

"They think the child is behind it?"

Kurt nodded.

I groaned. "Meisis has got nothing to do with it."

"As long as you can't prove it, they'll think something different."

"When will they come?" I asked.

"Not before tomorrow. The search isn't over yet."

He fumbled in his coat and brought out a pack of cigarettes from his inside pocket.

"Brought these for you."

"What do you want for them?"

"Nothing."

I was surprised. "Really?"

Kurt nodded and pressed the pack into my hand. I took out a cigarette.

"Do you want one?" I asked.

"Quit years ago."

I lit the cigarette and inhaled the smoke.

"Should I not have taken in the child?" I asked, after we'd been silently staring at the bottom of the pool for a while.

"If you hadn't taken it in, it would be dead already."

I tapped the ash from the cigarette. "Whether it's now or later, what's the difference?"

"They haven't come for the child yet. Who knows, sometimes unforeseen things happen."

"Like what?"

Kurt didn't say anything.

"I'm going to Eggert's," I said, passing him the burning cigarette and walking towards the house.

"Do you really think that's such a good idea?", Kurt called after me.

"We'll soon see," I called back.

I WON'T SURRENDER, BECAUSE I HAVE NOTHING TO LOSE.

40.

As I drove into Eggert's yard, the sheepdogs started barking. Next to house, the flag hung at half-mast. I took the cloth bag of Gösta's onions and got out. In the main house the front door opened, and Levaii came out.

"What do you want?" she shouted, her hand on the handle.

"I need clothes for the child. I can give you onions for them," I said, holding up the cloth bag.

Levaii's face looked tearstained. "You better go," she said.

I acted oblivious. "Is everything alright?"

Levaii threw a fearful look over her shoulder.

"What's going on?" I asked.

Eggert appeared behind Levaii. His expression darkened when he saw me.

"You!" he shouted. "You must be crazy showing your face here!"

"I don't understand what's going on," I said.

"Do you think I'm stupid?"

The dogs started barking again.

Levaii tugged on her father's sleeve. "Maybe she really doesn't know yet," she said.

Eggert climbed down the steps and came hobbling over to me. Sweat shone on his bald head.

"What's happened?" I asked.

"My sisters have disappeared," Levaii said.

"And you lot are responsible," Eggert said.

"What do you mean they've disappeared?" I asked.

"She really hasn't heard," Levaii said to her father, who suddenly seemed lost in the large yard.

"Their cars were found abandoned in different parts of

the territory," she told me. "And their rooms are empty, as if they'd never lived in them."

She went and stood beside her father.

"They're always walking around the territory," I said.

Levaii shook her head. "No one's seen them."

"They'll show up," I said.

"Do you think we're stupid," Eggert yelled, pushing me up against the pick-up. "Go ask that brat you found in the forest why my daughters aren't here anymore."

"You think Meisis is behind this?"

"Who else?"

"But Meisis was with me the whole time," I lied.

"That doesn't mean anything," he said, tightening his grip so that I could barely breathe.

"Let her go," Levaii said, and forced herself between us. Eggert let go of me only reluctantly. I rubbed my throat.

"For years we lived here in peace, then that brat showed up and now this. How can they not be connected, tell me that?"

I said nothing. Eggert wanted to come at me again, but Levaii held on to him tightly.

"This won't bring them back to us," she said to him.

"You have three days to deliver the child to us. Otherwise, I'm coming to get it," he said.

Levaii pulled him back to the house.

"Three days," he repeated.

I got back into the pick-up and rushed to drive out of the yard.

In the rearview mirror I saw them watching me. The sheepdogs began barking again. Even as I reached our house, I still had the feeling that I could hear them. The landscape lost its colour in the twilight.

Edith was listening out for me. She was standing ready in the hallway, the dogs at her side. Exhausted, I let the door snap shut behind me.

"What were you thinking taking off and leaving the child here?"

"Where's Meisis?"

"I put her to bed. She asked after you the whole time. Where were you?"

"Levaii's sisters have gone missing," I said.

Edith didn't seem surprised. "So now they have a reason?"

I stepped towards her. "What do you know about it?" I asked.

"Me?"

"Are you hiding something from me?"

"I saw them walking around."

"Levaii's sisters?"

She shook her head. "The ones looking for them. I knew something must have happened. They never usually come that close to our house. But I wasn't sure. I thought that maybe I'd just imagined it. It was hard making them out in the dim light."

"I saw them too."

Edith nodded. "Now they'll come, right?"

"Yes. There's nothing else I can do."

For a brief moment I thought that Edith was going to take a step towards me. She raised her arm, as if she wanted to reach out to me, but then she let it drop abruptly and stayed where she was.

"I told you it would come to this," she said.

IS LEAVING ALL WE HAVE IN THE END?

41.

Sleep was out of the question. I walked restlessly around the house. Edith sat in the light of the kitchen lamp and underlined individual sentences in the book lying in front of her on the table. She looked up searchingly every time I entered the room, but I didn't want to speak to her.

When the house felt too cramped, I went into the garden and leant against the plum tree. The bark scratched at my back. I tilted back my head and looked up at the branches. The blossoms were dried out. They would drop off over the next few days. Once again, there would be no plums.

I was heading to the shed to check on the nettle mulch I had prepared a few days before, when I heard something break in the undergrowth of the forest. I flinched and turned around. Between the trees I saw deer standing there. Quivering, with wetly gleaming, copper-coloured fur and rolling eyes. I didn't move, but they must have smelled me because they took flight and blundered back into the forest. I quickly turned and went into the shed. As I bent over the buckets of mulch under the workbench, the tin holding my milk teeth fell towards me. It was heavy in my hand. I carefully opened it.

For a long while I stared at the twenty teeth. They were overlaid with the sight of the fleeing deer.

There would be a party. I was sure of it. I had a plan.

I went up to Meisis's room. She was sleeping deeply.

I sat down beside her on the sofa and woke her up.

"Do you still have your milk teeth?" I asked.

Meisis looked at me confused.

I grabbed her by the shoulders. "Have your teeth already fallen out?"

She shook her head.

"Good," I said, "then go back to sleep."

I DREAMT EGGERT'S DAUGHTERS WERE FOUND IN THE FOREST. THEY HAD FALLEN ASLEEP IN A CLEARING. SIX GIRLS, ARRANGED IN A STAR FORMATION IN THE SUN-BLEACHED MOSS, TWITCHING EYEBALLS BEHIND THEIR CLOSED LIDS, THEIR SLEEP AS HEAVY AS THE FOG ONCE WAS.

I DREAMT THAT THEY HAD SPENT A WHOLE AFTERNOON DRINKING QUINCE SCHNAPPS BY THE RIVER, ONE BOTTLE AFTER THE OTHER AND THAT'S WHY THEY DIDN'T WAKE UP. THEY SLEPT THROUGH WHOLE DAYS AND DIDN'T NOTICE THE LIGHT CHANGING.

I DREAMT THAT THEY HID AWAY ON PURPOSE AND WANTED TO BE LOOKED FOR.

42.

That same night I drove to Gösta and Len. The lights were on in the house. I knocked, and Gösta let me in. She was wearing a white nightshirt that practically swallowed her body.

She led me to the kitchen. Len was sitting at the table and wasn't wearing her sunglasses. A milky haze lay over her irises. I squeezed her hand, and she smiled.

"I saw deer in the forest. Will there be a party?" I asked.

Gösta nodded.

"And they won't come to get the child until afterwards, right?"

"You know how important the parties are to them," Gösta said, passing me a glass of water.

"What do you have in mind?" Len asked me.

I didn't tell them, I didn't want to risk anything.

Before the bridge got been blown up, deer and wild boar often strayed into the territory on their flight from the coast. People rounded them up with their dogs and shot them in the road. Young girls slung on their rifles, just like their fathers had taught them. In the tiled kitchens the men butchered the animals, hung them to bleed out on the verandas of the balconies, and the following night everyone gathered on the party meadow, set up pavilions, fetched benches and tables and grilled the meat.

At midnight, when it was over, the first songs were intoned. This is how they sat together until the early hours of the morning. The children were there too, when their eyelids drooped, they were carried by their older brothers to the cars and laid down to sleep on the backseats.

"You know what, those were the good days," Gösta told me. "Back then there was nothing to be afraid of."

43.

I was standing shielded by the trees and looking towards the meadow where the party would be taking place. The pavilions had already been built; the white plastic coverings freshly washed. A grill was smoking. Cars and trucks were parked all over the place. Beer benches had been set up. I heard a couple of women laughing. Laid out on a wax tablecloth over a folding table were the skinned animals. Blood dripped into the grass.

Off to one side, next to the firepit, the children had gathered and stacked twigs and branches from the forest. I couldn't help but think that when it was lit they would lose control of it. Maybe a burning branch would come lose, slip out. The fire would spread in seconds. I saw the meadow ablaze.

But the children knew better. Before they shoved the lit match into the deadwood, they had a bucket of sand ready and had doused the ground with water.

Levke and Wolf were leaning against the canisters of homemade quince schnapps. In their hands they held clear plastic cups full of the brownish liquid, with which they repeatedly toasted one another.

The woman with the harsh face was there too. She stood off a little to the side, but in a way that nothing passed her by.

My eyes followed the dogs, which were hunting on the meadows. Not completely decided whether it was still a game or for real, they tumbled over one another and flashed their teeth. Behind the scenery, the sky had gone violet.

Len and Gösta used to sometimes take me to these parties, but I had always felt out of place. The other adults would punish me with suspicious looks or act as if I wasn't there. The children, too, only looked over every once in a while. Gösta and Len let me sit between them and gave me a bit of the meat when the others weren't looking.

The longer these evenings went on, the more everyone was drunk. When the first person fell backwards from the bench, I knew that it was best if I left, especially if Gösta and Len were already making their way home.

Once, I put it off for too long. A group of rowdy girls came up with the idea of pouring the schnapps out of their cups all over me. Luckily, only one of them was not yet drunk enough, all the others missed. Before they could come up with something new that they could do to me, I fled. At the house, I lay in the still full bathtub. The water was ice-cold. I only left the tub when I could no longer feel my body. I didn't breathe a word to Edith.

The older I became, the more I avoided the parties, until eventually I stopped going altogether. Sometimes I would still notice the distant glow of the fire when I walked through the forest at night, but I kept my distance.

Now I saw that nothing had changed since then. Only the faces of the people had become older. I couldn't find Gösta and Len anywhere.

With my chin up, I walked across the meadow to the pavilions. People stopped talking when they noticed me. I walked past the benches towards the grill, where Pesolt was standing with his back to me. Alerted by the spreading silence, he turned around.

"Well would you look at that, what an honour. We've missed having you here over the years. Did you bring the child with you? The grill's hot enough," he said, grinning.

I looked at him in silence.

"Just a joke." Pesolt laughed. "The three-day deadline isn't quite up yet."

"There's one thing all of you haven't considered with your allegation that Meisis is a changeling," I said.

Levke and Wolf filled their cups and came closer. A snide whistle came from another direction.

"Oh." Pesolt turned back to the grill and flipped the meat. "Didn't realise we were still debating."

The gathered people roared.

With a raised voice, I said: "Every child in this territory has lost their milk teeth, there's proof of this in their homes." I paused.

"But changelings don't lose their milk teeth. Their teeth always stay like a child's. That's how it was with Edith."

At the mention of Edith's name, Pesolt's face darkened.

"If Meisis is something not from here, like Edith, she won't lose her teeth," I said.

A few murmurs of agreement sounded from the beer benches. I continued my speech.

"The child is at the exact age when the replacing of teeth takes place. So when it happens, it's a sign that she's part of this territory, just like you."

I looked triumphantly at Pesolt. People got up from the beer benches in order to see better. The scene offered them a welcome diversion. I could tell from Pesolt's expression that he didn't trust me. But the tumult unleashed by what I had said couldn't be calmed. The wait for whether the child's teeth would fall out presented the prospect that there would finally be something for people to talk about again.

Pesolt turned to the grill, deep in thought. The hot coals made sweat run down his face. He rubbed the back of his neck, took the roasted meat from the grill with a fork, piled it on the readied plates and put fresh, still raw pieces on the grill. Their fat sizzled in the heat. He turned back to me and, with the prong of the fork, picked a piece of steak from between his teeth and spat it out at my feet. The others held their breath: they were waiting with excitement for what Pesolt would say.

"And your suggestion is now that we have to be patient? For months, years?" He laughed. The others joined in.

"Meisis's teeth will fall out soon," I said emphatically.

Pesolt turned to the others. "But we are all of the opinion, that Meisis," he spoke her name with disgust, "isn't a real child. This means we'll have to wait in vain, while this brat can continue its mischief-making."

The others nodded.

"Give us six months," I said. "If not even a single tooth has fallen out by then, I'll deliver the child to you."

"Six months is a very long time. Imagine all the bad things that could happen in the meantime."

"Four months would also be enough," I said quickly, "you'll see."

Pesolt put his face right in front of mine. I could see the burst blood vessels in his eyes.

"If anyone's going to decide how many months you get, it's me," he said so quietly that no one else could have heard it, and then louder for the others, he added: "Now that I think about it. A child, even if it's not from here, shouldn't die when it's innocent. Which is why I say we put up with it for two months. But if it hasn't lost any teeth by then, we'll go get it, because we should never get careless, even if we might have a child's life on our conscience. You understand that don't you?"

I wanted to respond, but I was interrupted by Eggert, who had staggered forward.

"I should wait two months?" he shouted. His mouth was

smeared with grease, his eyes were glassy. "What if that's too late for my daughters?"

Rumbling shouts from the back rows became louder.

"Meisis didn't have anything to do with the disappearance of your daughters," I said.

Eggert tried to punch me, but I moved easily out of his way. His movements were uncoordinated and slow from the schnapps. He lost his balance and fell to the ground. The woman with the stern face stepped out from the crowd and helped him up.

"Eggert's right," she said. "Even two months is too risky. We swore when we blew up the bridge that we wouldn't ever take anyone in ever again," she said, standing beside Eggert.

"I promise all of you that nothing will happen in the next two months," I said.

Pesolt laughed. The woman said, "It's not enough to just promise."

It fell quiet. All eyes were on us, mesmerised.

"If there is another incident, the child and I will leave the territory," I said.

The people on the benches began whispering amongst themselves.

The woman wanted to say something, but Pesolt cut her off.

'And Edith?" he said.

"What?"

"If something happens again, Edith must leave the territory too."

I could feel my pulse. Pesolt was once more holding the reins. Perhaps this was what he had intended to happen the whole time.

I straightened my shoulders and said: "You all have my word."

Pesolt's eyes glowed. "Say it properly."

I raised my hand. "Should something or other happen here that ought not to happen, Meisis, Edith and I will leave the territory."

"Good," Pesolt said. "We are, after all, civilised people. Eggert, you're in agreement with us, right?"

Everyone knew that it wasn't really a question. There wasn't anything left for Eggert to do but nod.

With this, Pesolt had uttered a decree. He leaned over to him and said: "If the child is guilty, it will get its rightful punishment. Then you'll also get your daughters back." He clapped him on the shoulder, and I could see that he was thrilled about planning the hunt for the next two months.

"Now, finally, let's drink," he said, grabbing his cup, the others followed his example.

"To the territory," he shouted.

"To our life," they responded, and knocked back the quince schnapps, their faces contorted with excitement. The hubbub started up again. I was no longer being observed.

Eggert stood up and tottered over to me.

"I'll kill that brat long before if you don't watch out," he hissed.

Pesolt stood behind him and put his arm around his shoulder. "It's OK, Eggert. The child won't slip through our fingers."

Eggert shook him off. "Since when have you been on Skalde's side?"

"Sleep off the schnapps first. Seems like you're not seeing things straight."

For a moment I thought Eggert was going to go for Pesolt,

but he just raised his hand, murmured something incomprehensible and stumbled back to his seat.

I wanted to steal away, but Pesolt turned to me and gripped my arm tightly.

"I warn you, don't get any ideas about doing something stupid, you hear me? And Edith better not get in our way either. And no little games with the dogs, understand? Otherwise, it may come to pass that your house accidently catches fire."

"I get it," I said.

Pesolt grinned and let me go. "Then everything's good."

I saw to it that I got away.

44.

Edith was lying in the tub in the bathroom.

"You smell of smoke," she said. "Where have you been?"

I leant forward over the wash basin and looked at myself in the mirror. I tried to smile, but it slipped out of place.

"The child's safe now," I said, turning around.

She creased her forehead. I told her about the party and what I was able to negotiate. Edith lifted her wet hair, twisted it into a bun, and squeezed the water out of it. "And what happens when Meisis's teeth don't fall out?"

"They will."

"How can you be so sure?"

"She's the right age."

"Mine never fell out."

I said nothing.

Edith sank back into the tub. Water flowed over the edge and ran over the tiles. "Sounds to me like all you've done is broker another deferral. And even if Meisis's teeth fall out, Pesolt will find a reason why she has to be handed over to him."

"Two months is a long time."

Edith watched the waves created by the movement of her body. "Have you thought for even a second that it's possible that Levaii's sisters haven't disappeared?"

"What do you mean by that?"

"Maybe they left voluntarily?"

"Where could they have gone?"

"You can't honestly believe that they just disappeared into thin air?"

"There must be a logical explanation. But they surely can't have left the territory by choice."

"How can you be so sure?"

"That would be suicidal. It's still only safe here in the territory.

"If that's what you think," Edith said. We avoided looking at one another. Our silence stood heavily between us.

"You have to lose your teeth," I said that evening to Meisis. We were sitting at the kitchen table eating thin onion soup. "If they fall out, you can stay here, in the house. With me and Edith."

Meisis's head sank and she turned her spoon over the tabletop. "And if they don't fall out?"

"Your teeth will fall out," I said firmly.

Meisis nodded, but something else seemed to be worrying her.

45.

My memories of the time after the party have a hazy shimmer.

I started showing Meisis the land. I woke her every morning, even before the sun had come up. We ate a meagre breakfast of dried roots, sometimes a few nuts, then we set off. I always showed her a different part of the territory. We hardly ever used the pick-up. I had missed walking, and I didn't want to have to keep to the roads.

In these early hours it was still bearable outside. We rarely rested and were constantly moving. When it got so hot in the morning that the asphalt on the road melted, we just lay in the shade.

For hours on end I walked with her through the territory and told her the specifics. I pointed at the fallen trees, the land line on the horizon, wild mustard, real verbena and musk mallow. The way the fieldstones were stacked in unshakeable formations. Three lone birches in an open field. The glowing orange rowan berries and the sandy soil.

I acted like there was nothing left to fear.

When the sun got even higher, we started back towards home. We fled inside the house. I hung up wet towels against the heat, but it hardly helped at all. We left the curtains closed the whole afternoon and dozed into the twilight.

In the evening, when I brought Meisis to bed, she said the names of the plants that I had shown her, quietly to herself, until she fell asleep.

"You should stop teaching her things that she can't use, in the end you're giving her false hope," Edith said, but I didn't listen to her.

During our wanderings it occurred to me that everything would become even dryer. The meadows and the fallow fields reminded me of the descriptions of the steppes that Edith read to me once a long time ago.

The yellowish-brown grass, the almost leafless bushes and trees. Their branches cut into the blue sky with their sharp edges.

Then once more whole processions of hedgerows in bloom. We could already smell them from far off. This idyll had something brutal about it. The scent pressed itself against my forehead and made me giddy.

The landscape seemed quieter to me too. The air was motionless. The vibrating chirps of the insects seemed to be sunken in the meadows.

Despite everything I still assumed that it was only a matter of time until this endless summer came to an end. I often imagined how I would lead Meisis through the misty landscape. I pictured us walking in two identical raincoats through wet meadows, the blue sky hidden behind thick clouds. The light dulled, bushes and trees a lush dark green. Water dripping from their branches.

I still see this in my dreams.

46.

Meisis enjoyed going into the forest with me more than anything.

Sometimes we would lie for hours between the pines and not move. It almost felt like we would sink into the landscape. Then I would imagine what it would be like to never get up again. How long would it take until our bodies could no longer be discerned from the surrounding nature?

We didn't find seagulls. They didn't fall from the sky as often as they used to. I told Meisis about how, as a child, I was always on the search for them in the forest. I usually struck it lucky when the wind came from the north. What I didn't tell Meisis was that I had to hide the gulls from Edith. Once, when she caught me in the act, she beat me black and blue. For her, even hunger wasn't a reason to eat the birds.

Each time before we went into the forest, Meisis would ask me for a rusk. During our wanderings she would put it on a tree stump not far from our house. When I asked her about it, she said: "For the animals."

I didn't stop her from doing it, even though I was certain that the forest was as empty as if someone had turned it upside down and shaken out every living thing.

Shortly afterwards, I was proven wrong. We found a cat in a thorny snow bush. Burdock in her fur. She hissed loudly as we pushed the branches to one side.

All the cats disappeared from the houses shortly after the bridge was blown up, Len had told me. Even saucers filled to the brim with milk placed in front of people's doors couldn't lure them back, they remained in the woodland. Until this day I had thought that they had all perished long ago.

"Careful it doesn't bite you," I said to Meisis.

Stooping, she moved closer to the cat and gently called to it. To my amazement the cat stopped arching its back. Meisis crouched down in front of it, and it thrust its head against her hand.

"Come on now," I said and pulled her onwards. The tame cat made me uneasy, and I wanted to get out of the forest as quickly as possible, but it followed us and prowled, mewing, around Meisis's legs.

"Can we take it home?" she asked.

I shook my head. "It will be dead soon," I said, without looking at Meisis. 'It doesn't belong in any house."

47.

Edith no longer slept the whole day. Instead, she lay on the sofa and read. Despite this, she was scarcely available to talk to. Once I found her in the kitchen, three open books in front of her. The pages were cut in places where there used to be pictures of the sea. Her hair hung in her face, it shone, freshly combed. I leant over her.

"Why are you sneaking around like that!"

"What are you reading?" I asked.

"Oh, nothing." Edith shut the books.

"Oh yeah."

"I was at the river," Edith said.

"You left the plot?" I asked.

She nodded, rooted around in her coat pocket and lay a small gold ring in front of her on the dark wood of the table. "Know what that is?"

I shook my head and asked: "What are you getting at?"

Edith gave me an urgent look. "I'm now almost completely sure that Levaii's sisters left of their own accord."

I sat down opposite Edith. "And you know this from a ring?"

"They wanted to leave something behind. Who could blame them."

I screwed up my mouth. "You don't really believe that do you?"

"Who else would choose to leave behind their gold ring on the bank? Tell me that."

"And now I should run to Pesolt with the ring, as proof that Meisis is innocent? He'll laugh at me."

"That's not what I meant."

"What else did you think the ring would be good for?"

Edith went quiet. Her look was dismissive.

"You're right, why am I mixing myself up in this. I didn't take in the child. I don't care what happens to it."

IN MY HEAD I SEE EDITH, AROUND HER THE DARKNESS AS RICH AS HER COAT, AND ONLY HER FACE ILLUMINATED BY THE LIGHT OF THE KITCHEN LAMP. I STAND BEFORE HER, AND ACROSS THE SCRATCHED WOOD OF THE TABLE SHE PUSHES SIX GOLD RINGS TOWARDS ME, ALWAYS THE SAME SCENE AGAIN, AN ENDLESS REPETITION, UNTIL I BEND FORWARD AND PUSH THE RINGS ONTO MY FINGERS, HANDS NOW TWICE AS HEAVY.

48.

WE SAW THE WATER. THE CHILD WAS WITHOUT FEAR.
IT SEEMED TO BE AFRAID OF NOTHING.

I also showed Meisis the river. We went along the stony bank and after a short time we reached what remained of the concrete bridge. Meisis paused, staring. It also occurred to me for the first time how unreal the whole thing looked. The end of the bridge jutted out into emptiness. Beneath it: deep water, a strong current. The other bank was far off.

"Can we go up there?" Meisis asked. I looked around, no one was in sight, and I nodded. We climbed up and walked to the road that led to the bridge. Weeds grew in the cracks in the asphalt. Some places were grimy, boulders both large and small lay all around. Without hesitating, Meisis went further. I followed her. Before she could step even closer to the edge, I grabbed her by the collar.

"If you fall, you're lost," I said. "Ove, Pesolt's first wife, went that way."

Meisis only reluctantly took a couple of steps back.

I remembered the incident like a story from one of Edith's books. One night, Ove had sleepwalked to the bridge and had fallen. People later said they had seen Ove standing in their front garden under the elderflower bush only in her nightshirt. But when they stepped outside, Ove was already gone and there was nothing to indicate in which direction she had disappeared.

Kurt found her the next day. They only just managed to get her out of the river.

The images in which I imagine this all have bleached-out colours. I was ten, maybe eleven, when the incident occurred.

I still clearly remember people wore black for months and everyone cut the flowers from their gardens and brought them to Ove's grave.

On one of the first nights after Ove's death, Pesolt drove to our house and parked his car with the engine running and the headlights on in our driveway. The light fell through the curtains and lit up the inside of the house. I huddled under the stairs next to the dogs. Edith was sitting crossed legged in the living room on the sofa.

At some point Pesolt got out and shouted in front of the house: "What did you whisper in her ear, you cursed woman."

At this, Edith jumped up, staggered passed me through the corridor, threw open the front door and stood in the glaring light of the headlights.

"Are you really suggesting that I'm responsible for the death of your wife?" she shouted, shaking all over. This was followed by a deep silence. Then Pesolt climbed back in his car and drove off.

Edith shut the door behind her and went into the kitchen. I followed her. She had sat at the kitchen table and for the first time she let me surmise her pain. Following a reflex, I touched her. Edith looked up and looked at me. In a lightening quick movement, she grabbed me and rammed her knife into my hand. I was so shocked that in the first few moments I didn't feel any pain. I single drop of blood ran down my hand. Edith casually pulled the blade back out.

"You'll need to put pressure on that," she said, wiping the knife on her coat and leaving. I looked at the wound, which had begun to bleed heavily. It was as if it wasn't my hand. From the dresser drawer I fetched a dishcloth and wrapped it tightly around the wound. I felt dizzy and had to prop myself up on the window sill. From there I saw Edith walk through the back door, fetch the axe from the shed and begin hacking up wood we would never need.

Edith could never forgive the fact that Pesolt blamed her for Ove's death.

I later learned from Kurt that Ove used to regularly disappear at night when she was still only a child. Once Pesolt found her the next day in the quarry. She was standing completely still on a flat white rock that marked the middle of the pit.

Another time, Wolf and Levke had discovered her around noon in an abandoned barn. She was lying there in the straw sleeping with her eyes open, in her hand, the remains of a mouse.

As a child, Ove had done things that she couldn't remember afterwards. She had started sleepwalking after the bridge had been blown up, but no one wanted to see the connection.

After Ove and Pesolt had got married, she seemed to be better for a while, but as the weather started to turn, the attacks came back.

Once, she came to our house and had kept knocking until Edith let her in. From my hiding place under the stairs, I watched the two women standing opposite one another in the hallway. Edith in her black rabbit fur coat, thick woollen socks, her bright hair twisted into a knot, her back arched. Ove with a woollen hat, dirty rubber boots, wide-fit jeans and a yellow raincoat, which was dripping water onto the floor and forming a puddle. They both, in their own ways, looked undaunted.

"I heard you sew coats," Ove asked and held out her hand. Edith folded her arms over her chest. I could see that she thought Ove was making fun of her.

"Why do you want to know?"

Ove laughed. "I'd very much like to have one."

"What do I get out of it?"

"Two dogs have shown up at ours. Great Danes. My husband doesn't want them. I would give them to you."

"What would I do with dogs?"

"I thought you had a knack with them. When you arrived, they –"

Edith interrupted her. "And you want a coat?"

"Yes, one would be enough."

Edith nodded. "I'll go get them."

Ove turned to me. I pushed myself deeper into the shadow of the stairs. She smiled at me, but I was so scared I didn't move.

Edith came back and led Ove into the kitchen. Through the open door I saw the way she spread the coats out on the table. After long consideration, Ove decided on one with broad sleeves and a hem that reached the floor.

"The dogs are in the car. I'll go get them" she said, and left.

While waiting, Edith paced back and forth in the corridor.

Ove came back inside with the dogs in her arms. She put the puppies on the floor. They walked, yapping, over to Edith, who crouched down and held out her hand to them.

"Do you like them?"

Edith nodded. The two women shook hands and Ove left the house with the coat.

She came to ours a couple of times after this. Her and Edith withdrew into the kitchen, where they spoke to each other in whispers. I eavesdropped at the door, but I couldn't make out a single word.

Meisis took one more look over the edge at the water, before we climbed down from the bridge together. Below on the bank I tried to show her how to skim stones, but the waves were too high, and they only sunk.

"What's on the other side?" Meisis asked.

I looked over. The distance seemed insurmountable. The water looked menacing. It drew stones into itself from the bank over and over again. And yet, on the other side grew the same bushes, and even further off, a pine forest began.

"That's a different territory. If you walk far enough, you get to the sea. But it's not safe over there," I said.

"Why's it not safe there?" Meisis asked.

"There's no more houses over there, nowhere you could find shelter, no provisions and no one who could help you."

The answer didn't seem to satisfy Meisis, she kept staring steadfastly at the other side.

"Show me your teeth," I said quickly, and turned her chin towards me. "Are any of them wobbly?"

Meisis probed her mouth with her tongue. She shook her head.

I threw a stone. It sunk like a shot bird.

"We should head back," I said, taking her hand.

Together we climbed the embankment to the top. Meisis turned one more time to the river and waved farewell to it.

49.

Once, I thought I saw Meisis walking through the garden at night, barefoot, her face hidden in the darkness. Then the shadows swallowed her up. I forgot about it, in the belief that I had only imagined her red head of hair, climbed up to the attic and went to sleep. The image got lost in a dream.

It wasn't until much later that I remembered it again.

50.

A few days later I noticed one of Edith's mother-of-pearl bracelets on Meisis's wrist. I gripped her tightly and said, "She doesn't like it when other people wear her jewellery, put it back before she notices."

Meisis pulled out of my grip. "She gave it to me," she said.
"No she didn't."
Meisis nodded. "I was allowed to choose something."
"Don't take it outside, you'll only lose it," I said.

Edith had always forbidden me from taking something from her jewellery box, and threatened to stab the tires on the pick-up if she ever caught me with her jewellery.

Later, I was digging a new bit of the garden for the potato patch, and Meisis came to me wanting to help.

"I don't need any help," I said, and turned my back to her. Meisis made herself scarce underneath the plum tree and played with the building blocks. From the corner of my eye I could see that she kept raising her head and looking at me, but I acted as though I hadn't noticed.

In the evening Edith came into the kitchen, got herself some of the soup I'd cooked and sat with us at the table.

"What's up?" I asked her.
"Am I not allowed to eat?"
"You never eat."
"Of course I do."
"But I never see you eating."
"You don't have eyes everywhere you know."

Meisis sat up in her chair. "I've seen Edith eating quite often."

"Oh yeah, what does Edith eat then?" I asked, leaning across the table towards Meisis.

"Potatoes, meat…"

Edith grinned. "You see."

Meisis went to sleep straightaway that evening. All four limbs stretched out on the sofa bed, breathing deeply. I looked at her unsuspecting face, leaned over and gently pulled the bracelet off her wrist. I quietly left the room, climbed downstairs and went into the garden. I pushed my way through the high grass up to the bramble bush and entered the forest. In the bright moonlight it wasn't hard to find the tree stump where Meisis always put a rusk. I placed the bracelet in the middle of the flat cut surface and walked back to the house.

The following day, Meisis looked for the bracelet.

"I still had it when I went to sleep last night," she said. She asked Edith too. I had a firm expectation that Edith would react indignantly, but instead she calmly listened to Meisis, staring outside into the garden, where the abandoned pool sliced into the landscape. Without looking away she said to Meisis that she could simply pick out something new.

In the night I went back to the spot in the forest. But the bracelet was no longer there. I looked at the ground too, pushed aside branches and felt around in the moss, but I couldn't find it there either.

51.

The next morning I saw Edith walking into the garden with a bucket, cloth and soap. I didn't think much of it, made Meisis breakfast and went back to bed.

When I got up around midday, Edith had cleaned the pool.

It glowed blue in the bright light. The high, dry grass was almost colourless in comparison. Edith was filling it with water from the garden hose. She was wearing her fur coat, a grey satin dress and gold earrings with sections made from mother-of-pearl. Only her lips, cracked by the heat, didn't fit the image. Meisis was squatting at her feet. She looked fixedly at the running water. Nearby, the dogs dozed in the shade.

"Great, isn't it?" Edith asked, as I headed towards them through the garden. I stood next to her. Meisis raised her eyes only briefly.

"I'm going to teach her how to swim," Edith said, and tugged up the sleeve of her coat. The sun was at its highest point in the sky. The air was a thick mass. I felt light-headed.

"Why would it be great? I asked, wiping the sweat from my brow.

Edith twisted her mouth. "I taught you too."

"And what did I get from it? The other children just thought I was even weirder."

"But Meisis wants to learn," Edith said.

For a moment I pictured very clearly pushing Edith's head under water in the half-filled pool. She wouldn't be able to get free from my grip. How long does it take for someone to drown?

"Is that true?" I asked Meisis.

"It's so hot," she replied. I pressed my lips together.

Edith turned to her. "Right, in with you."

Meisis got up and looked into the pool. There were already a couple of dead flies floating on the surface of the water.

"Don't be coy," said Edith. Meisis slowly climbed down the steps. This far in, the water came up to her knees.

"I'm scared," she said, stopping.

"What of?", Edith said.

"It feels weird."

"You have to go to the middle," Edith said, but Meisis stayed where she was. I grinned. Edith turned to me.

"What if you go in too?" Her voice was suddenly very soft. I didn't know when she last asked me to do something.

"Fine," I said, getting out of my trousers and t-shirt and into the pool. When I reached Meisis, she clung onto me. In the water she was even lighter than before.

I looked at Edith. "And now?"

"You have to move like a frog, have you forgotten?" She showed us.

"You have to stand here in the pool," I said, but went further in with Meisis, the bottom of the pool dropped away.

The water came up to my shoulders.

"Dive under?" I asked quietly.

She nodded.

"Three, two, one."

I pulled our weight under water and breathed out. Air bubbles rose to the surface. I fought against the buoyancy. How long does it take for someone to drown?

Meisis's grip became tighter. Her fingernails cut into my skin. My chest tightened. The only thing I could hear was my own heartbeat.

Meisis tried to go back to the surface, but I wouldn't let her go. Staying underwater suddenly seemed completely logical to me. I closed my eyes. Hands grabbed us and pulled us up.

Meisis wheezed. Her eyes were red. Edith released her from my arms and lifted her out of the pool. Water dripped from her fur. Meisis cowered shaking in the grass.

I bit my lower lip so hard I tasted blood and climbed out of the pool.

"What were you thinking?" Edith asked me.

"I must have forgotten how to swim."

Meisis looked between us back and forth. Water beaded in her hair.

"I've changed my mind, I don't want to learn anymore," she said, standing up and walking into the house. The dogs followed her, as if they had to protect Meisis from us.

THE WATER IN THE POOL REFLECTS THE SKY, THE SURFACE LOOKS STABLE, AND YET I LOST MY GRIP.

52.

I sat on the edge of the bath while Meisis stood on the footstool in front of the wash basin brushing her teeth. I didn't let her out of my sight while she did so and when she had finished and was about to walk past me out of the bathroom, I grabbed onto her and gripped her chin.

"Have you checked your teeth?" I asked.Meisis shook her head. I pushed her back to the wash basin and put her back on the stool. She leaned so far forward that her nose almost touched the mirror and she felt every tooth, but none of them wobbled. She dropped her hands and vacantly looked herself in the eyes. She suddenly seemed much older. I had to look away.

I opened the window in her room, Meisis rolled into a ball on the bed. I sat down next to her. Light fell into the room from the corridor, but her face lay in shadow.

She reached for my hand.
"Will it hurt when I lose my teeth?" she asked.
"When it's time, they come out just as easily as the bones come out of the rabbit after we've been boiling it all day," I answered.
"But the rabbit is dead when that happens."
"You have nothing to be scared of."
"Why does Edith still have her milk teeth?"
"I don't know."
"What will happen if mine don't fall out?"
I put the covers over Meisis. "Sleep now, it's late."
"Can you stay with me tonight?" she asked.
I nodded and fetched my blanket from the attic.

Meisis's uneasy sleep rubbed off on me. I felt the cool wall behind me. I tried to keep my eyes closed, but I couldn't. Meisis sat up in bed. She felt around for me.

"Go back to sleep," I said, trying to push her back down onto the mattress, but Meisis shook her head.

"I'm too hot," she whispered.

I passed her the water bottle from the night table. With only half-open eyes, she unscrewed the lid and drank in large, hurried gulps.

"I dreamt that Edith disappeared," she said, "we looked everywhere, but we didn't even find her coat."

"Edith isn't going to disappear," I said.

"Are you sure?"

"She's sleeping on the sofa like she always does."

"Can you go check?"

"That really isn't necessary."

"Please."

I got up with a groan and felt around in the dark for the door.

"Try to go back to sleep."

In the corridor, the light flickered. I walked barefoot across the floorboards.

The living room was deserted. In the place where Edith always lay, there was a hollow in the sofa. In the kitchen there was a half-empty glass of water on the table.

I went back upstairs and paused at the window. Three dead flies on the sill. Their black, armour-like bodies were withered up. I was tempted to squash them with my thumbnail. Instead, I looked outside where the pick-up was sitting in the light of the moon. Inside it, I saw Edith. I turned on my heel.

Outside, the air was as sticky as it was inside. I slowly walked down the sand path to the pick-up.

Edith was sitting and staring behind the steering wheel, her hands in her lap. I opened the door and shuffled into the passenger seat. A quiet crackling was coming from the speakers of the car radio.

"Meisis is looking for you" I said.

Edith turned her head. She had painted her lips so dark, they looked black.

"I wanted to listen to music, but the stupid thing is broken," she said. She hit the radio with her palm.

"It's late, you should go to sleep," I said, but she didn't respond.

"We could get away from here. You, the child and me," she said instead.

"What are you talking about?" I asked.

"It's not safe here anymore."

"I won't leave here, and neither will the child."

"Did you know that the other side of the river is no different to this one?" she asked, gripping the wheel.

"I'm not interested in the other side," I said. Edith blinked.

"Even the dogs are smarter than you," she said.

I felt the need to run and hide, but my body didn't obey me. Instead, I just sat there.

Edith cleared her throat. "I'm going to lie down," she said, and climbed out of the pick-up.

I still couldn't move. In my ears swelled the crackling from the speakers of the radio, it screwed painfully into my ear canal.

Maybe this was the moment I realised I hadn't had things under control for a long time.

53.

THE DOGS DISAPPEARED ON THE DAY WE THOUGHT THERE WAS GOING TO BE A STORM. AROUND MIDDAY THE SKY HAD TAKEN ON AN ALMOST BLACK HUE. THE STUFFY AIR CRACKLED WITH ELECTRICITY.

Nothing stirred. Meisis and I paced back and forth in the garden and waited for the rain. The dogs had come outside with us, but I barely paid any attention to them, I never did. I didn't feel responsible. When we went back into the house, I didn't notice that the dogs hadn't followed us in.

There wasn't a storm. The sky simply cleared again.

Edith was the first to notice their absence.

"We're going to go look for them right now," she said, sounding strangely calm.

All three of us walked through the forest together. Edith whistled inaudibly, so high, that it hurt my ears. Meisis looked in every bush. I checked the meadows with binoculars, but we didn't find the dogs.

"Maybe they've been back home for a while already," I said to try and comfort Edith.

We made our way home. When we had almost reached the plot, I noticed that Meisis was no longer walking behind us. I stood there and called her name, but I could only hear the echo of my own voice.

"She was still there a moment ago," Edith said, stroking her sweaty hair out of her face.

I looked around frantically. Nothing moved in the forest. I wanted to go back along the route that we had just taken, but Edith held my arm tightly.

"She'll show up in a minute," she said.

We waited, but nothing happened. I was seized by panic. I was already imagining how Eggert had waylaid Meisis and was now pressing his hand over her mouth. At that moment, Meisis's red hair appeared between the trees. She walked slowly, all the while looking left and right.

"You can't scare us like that," I shouted, and grabbed her by the shoulders.

She looked at me surprised.

"Never do that again." I pulled her towards me.

"What were you thinking?" Edith asked.

"I wanted to make sure that we hadn't missed anywhere," Meisis said.

"But we already looked there," I said. Meisis didn't say anything.

After I had brought her to bed that evening, I went to see Edith in the living room. She was lying on the sofa and reading.

"Do you think Meisis had something to do with the dogs disappearing?" I asked.

She put down the book and looked at me. "Is that what you think?"

I balled my hands up into fists and stared at my knuckles.

"No, why would she?" I asked, but I didn't sound as decisive as I would have liked.

"She's just a child. You shouldn't let yourself get upset so easily," Edith said, reopening the book.

54.

The supplies that I had been hoarding for years depleted. Meisis was always hungry. Sometimes I would find her between mealtimes in the pantry, a rusk or a piece of dried fruit in her hand. She was never satisfied by what I gave her. I counted the tins, the potatoes, over and over again, cooked thinner soups. There were still the rabbits at least. Apart from Len and Gösta, no one wanted to exchange things with me anymore. They wouldn't even open the door when I stood outside with canisters of mulch. As long as Meisis still had her milk teeth, no one trusted me. And I couldn't do anything about it.

55.

Ever since the dogs had gone missing, Meisis didn't want to sleep alone in her room anymore, which is why I moved in with her completely.

One night, we were woken by dogs barking. It sounded like they were under our window. Meisis hid under the covers. I threw open the window in the hope of seeing the dogs in the garden, but nothing was there, and the barking had fallen silent.

When I opened my eyes in the morning, Edith was sitting on the floor next to the sofa. I sat bolt upright, startled. Meisis was sleeping peacefully. "It wasn't the dogs," Edith said. "Just some other dogs."

I rubbed my eyes. "You saw them?" I asked.

Edith nodded. "They still listen to me."

"It's not a good idea for you to start luring the dogs here again. Pesolt is waiting for any excuse to get us."

Edith glared at me angrily. "I have to find the dogs. I'll do whatever it takes."

There was nothing I could say.

56.

Levaii arrived on our plot as the sun was at its peak.

Meisis had curled up to nap in the bathroom, I had laid out her covers on the cold tiles. Edith was sleeping in a ball on the sofa. The sheet like a shroud over her face.

I was standing in the pantry, inspecting the supplies. Meisis and I brought back anything edible we found on our walks, but it was not enough. Even finding grass for the rabbits was becoming more and more difficult due to the extreme humidity.

I heard the muffled sound of a bicycle bell from outside.

Levaii let her bike fall in the sand out front and came up to the house out of breath. Her grey t-shirt was drenched in sweat.

"What do you want?" I called from the door.

"Can I come in?"

I shook my head. "Best you didn't."

Levaii puffed a strand of hair out of her face and dropped her arms to her side.

"I have to get out of the sun, otherwise I'll get heatstroke."

"Let's go into the garden. There's shade there," I said, leading her around the house.

Levaii stopped next to the pump and operated the lever. She lowered her head and let the water run over the back of her neck and her hands and she gulped some down.

"Do you get the feeling it's getting hotter every day?" she asked, blinking up at me.

"It can't keep going on like this," I replied, mentally noting that I sounded like Gösta.

We sat under the plum tree. Yawning, Levaii leant against

the trunk. I took a cigarette out of the breast pocket of my shirt, stuck it between my lips and lit it up.

"So, what's this about?" I asked, inhaling the smoke.

"My father wants to make you an offer, that you, as he said, 'cannot refuse'"

"What kind of offer?"

"He wouldn't tell me. You have to come to our barn tomorrow night."

She looked transfixed at my cigarette, but I acted as if I didn't notice.

"Has it got something to do with your sisters?"

Levaii shrugged her shoulders. "Probably. He doesn't talk about anything else. He even keeps saying their names in his sleep."

"Do you think the child is responsible for their disappearance?" I asked.

Levaii didn't say anything, then she said. "I'm not sure."

I lowered the hand holding the cigarette.

"They said some strange things," she added.

"What kind of things?"

"That blowing up the bridge was the wrong thing to do. They said that they'd go crazy, just like Ove, because they can only go around in circles here."

She picked up a leaf that was lying on the ground next to her and shredded it between her fingers.

"I always thought it was just a turn of phrase," she said.

"And Eggert?"

Levaii waved her hand. "He's fully convinced that the child's behind it. Let's stop talking about it, I've told you what I was supposed to pass on." She stood up. I got up too.

"Are you sure you want to ride back in this heat?"

"I don't have any other choice, or are you going to let me in the house now after all?" Levaii grinned.

I didn't return the smile and said: "Tell Eggert that I'll be there tomorrow."

57.

Meisis and I were awoken in the night by the bright light of a torch shining into the room from outside. I lay on my back and didn't move. Meisis felt for my hand and held it so tightly it hurt. The light began to flicker, then went out, only to once more wander across the bedcovers. Sleeping was out of the question.

It was only when I leant out of the window and yelled that it remained dark.

58.

Eggert's barn stood brightly lit in the night. It sat behind the pasture where he used to keep his cows until they all died on him. The light fell on the scorched lawn through the open door. I went inside. It smelled of straw and animals. The sweat collected on my top lip. The heat was now oppressive at night too. Eggert was standing in the middle of the barn. The light of the halogen lamp reflected off of his bald head. He had unbuttoned his shirt. For the first time I saw the tattoos on his chest. Listed below one another were the seven names of his daughters. Levaii's last.

He greeted me with a nod and indicated that I should sit opposite him on a folding chair. I reluctantly complied with his request.

"I want to make you an offer," he said.

"Levaii told me. What's the offer?"

"You'll get something from me, but to get it you have to hand over the brat to me."

I leaned back in the chair. "I wouldn't hand over Meisis for anything in the world," I said.

"Listen to what I have to say to you first."

I crossed my arms across my chest. Eggert looked at me intensely.

"You know about my petrol supply. If you give me the child now, I'll share it with you."

I laughed.

"But that's not all. I'll turn over half of my supply to you. And on top of that I'll protect you."

"Protect me from what?"

"Pesolt. You don't really think he'll just leave you in peace when the child's eliminated, do you?"

"What are you talking about?"

"You haven't kept to the rules. He'll never be able to look the other way, but I'll make sure that he leaves you and Edith in peace."

"And for that I should give you Meisis?"

Eggert nodded. I leaned forward.

"Listen Eggert, Meisis is not responsible for the disappearance of your daughters. She won't be able to bring them back to you."

Eggert laughed. "Let me worry about that."

"And what if they left here of their own free will?" I said, and for a moment my voice seemed to hang in the air.

"What did you say?"

"The river –" I began, but Eggert interrupted me.

"The bridge is destroyed, the river can't be crossed."

"Maybe they swam? Edith thinks –"

"Are you completely nuts? No one here can swim. And why would they even try? We've got everything here. We're on the right side." Eggert's voice cracked.

I bit my lip. "The child is innocent. She can't bring your daughters back."

Eggert looked around filled with hate. "You'll regret this."

I stood up. Eggert stepped towards me and put his face very close to mine.

"My daughters are no traitors, understand?" he said.

I nodded, but I made it clear to him with the look in my eyes that I believed something different. Before things got dangerous, I turned around and walked out of the barn, into the dark night.

WHICH BONDS WOULD REMAIN IF I WERE TO FORGET AN EMBER IN THE STRAW? THE FLAMES WOULD BE SEEN FOR MILES AROUND.

59.

The following day, Eggert brought the dead dogs to our house.

From the window halfway up the stairs, I watched how he parked his Range Rover on the sand path, got out and opened the trunk. In a workmanlike way, he heaved first one and then the other dog out and lay them in front of our door. Whistling, he closed the trunk.

"What did you do to them?" I shouted. Eggert turned to me.

"A little gift."

"They're Edith's dogs. She's got nothing to do with the child."

"My daughters don't have anything to do with the child, either, and yet they've disappeared," he said. Then he got back in his car and drove off.

Edith didn't say a word while she walked around the dogs. I barely dared to breathe. Meisis leaned against me, she didn't hide her grief. Edith abruptly stopped walking.

"Damn Eggert," she said, and I could hear how difficult it was for her to keep her voice from shaking. "If he dares come to our house again, I'll drown him in the pool with my own hands."

We buried the dogs in the garden where the brambles were. Edith wore a black silk dress under her rabbit fur coat and had given us black things to wear too. Our sweat made them even darker. How Edith could bear it in her fur coat remains a mystery to me. After we had filled in the holes, she read several poems while standing in the blazing sun. Her chin raised. More angry than sad.

"Do you remember how I told you that it wasn't safe here anymore?" Edith asked me that evening. "Now you can no longer deny it. When the two months are up, they won't treat us any differently than the dogs."

"It's only Eggert that's lost his mind. He acted alone."

"How do you know that?"

"Gösta would never agree to anything like that."

"You're so naïve."

I didn't respond.

"We should leave the territory while we still can."

"Meisis and I aren't going anywhere."

"You really think that it's enough to just sit out the whole thing, don't you?"

"As if we have any other choice."

60.

THE SEAGULLS HAVE BEEN FALLING FROM THE SKY FOR YEARS, LOSING THEIR GRIP ON THE HORIZON, PLUNGING FEATHERS.

It was the first windy day in a long time. While standing in the garden, I stretched my hand into the air.

"Today we'll go into the forest and look for seagulls," I told Meisis. "Put your shoes on."

I fetched a plastic bag from the kitchen.

We spent the whole morning looking through the undergrowth, but it wasn't until around midday that we made a find. The gull had become trapped in a rose hip bush. Meisis cried out when she found it. It couldn't have fallen that long ago, its body was still warm.

"Great," I said to her, and stowed the bird in the plastic bag

We roamed the forest for a while longer, but we didn't find a second gull.

"Let's go back," I said to Meisis, "before it gets any hotter."

Back at the house I lay the waxcloth over the table and showed her how to pluck a seagull.

Edith came and stood stunned in the doorframe. "What are you doing?"

"We found a seagull," Meisis said proudly.

Edith looked at me. "What have I told you about seagulls?"

"They fall from the sky, we didn't kill this one," I said.

"It really wasn't alive anymore," Meisis said, coming to my defence.

"I don't give a crap," shouted Edith, "In my house we don't eat seagulls."

"Do you really think we can still be picky? If you don't want to eat them, fine, but Meisis and I aren't going to starve."

"You're no different than the rest of the people here," Edith said and slammed the door behind her.

Later, after I had reassured Meisis and brought her to bed, I went to Edith, who was in the living room lying on the sofa.

I pushed a few clothes to one side and sat on the floor next to her.

"I consulted your books," I said. "The seagulls come from the sea. And they can't stay up in the air because they no longer have the strength. That's obvious. But you want to go to the exact place where the seagulls are fleeing from? And you remember the animals that always end up here? Gösta says that they come from the sea too, she can taste it, their meat is saltier than our animals."

Edith didn't move, I carried on speaking: "Meisis and I are staying here. But if you want to hold onto the idea of getting away from here, we won't stop you."

I got up and left the room without looking back.

61.

The next day, Edith slaughtered all of the rabbits. The kitchen was filled with the smell of blood. Edith sat hunched over the table. Before her lay the skinned white pelts. Using her knife, she removed the flesh and fat from the underside. The dead animals lay in the sink. The meat shimmered red. I opened my mouth, but no sound came out.

"You never forget how to butcher an animal," Edith said.

"Is that all of the rabbits?" I asked.

Edith raised her head. "They weren't coping with the heat. Three of them were already dead."

I looked at her, aghast. "But what do you want the fur for?"

"I'm making a coat for the child."

"You've gone crazy."

Edith laughed. "I don't know what's so crazy about it."

"No? Then please explain to me why Meisis would need a fur coat in this weather?" I was outwardly still very calm.

"It will be cold by the sea."

"Don't start that again."

Edith made a stubborn face.

"What are we supposed to eat now?" I asked.

Edith's movements became erratic. "For goodness' sake, the pantry and the cellar are full. And we've still got the potato patch. I really don't see what the problem is."

"But that won't last forever. We relied on the meat," I was now shouting, but Edith still didn't want to understand. I grabbed her by the hair and pulled back her head. "You only did this because Meisis and I ate the seagull," I said, "you wanted to get back at me."

"Let go, you're hurting me."

I wanted to throw something, wanted to shatter Edith's skull, but what good would it have done?

62.

A few days later, Meisis and I were digging up the potato patch and covering the soil with mulch, when I heard a sound in the forest.

"Who's there?" I shouted, pushing Meisis behind me.

"Only me," Kurt said, coming out from behind the brambles. Hanging from his braids were leaves and twigs, maybe he had plaited them in.

"Is Edith home?" he asked, waving at Meisis.

"She's sleeping," I said.

"I have to talk to her."

I told Meisis to let Edith know. She nodded and walked into the house.

I lit a cigarette. The smoke scratched my throat, and my eyes watered. "What do you want with Edith?" I asked.

"She wanted me to find out something for her."

"When did you speak to each other?"

"The last time I was here. You'd driven to Eggert's, remember? Shortly after you'd left, she came to me."

I looked at him mistrustfully. "And what was it you had to find out for her?"

Kurt didn't get around to answering me. Edith had appeared in the doorway and called out: "Thought you'd finally defected to the animals."

He laughed. "I thought about it," he said.

"Come in." Edith waved him over.

I held Kurt's arm tightly. "What plan's she hatching?" I asked him quietly.

"I'll tell you later," Kurt said. "But don't worry."

He went to Edith and disappeared into the house with her.

It was only when I went into the kitchen making soup from yesterday's leftovers that Kurt and Edith came out of the living room.

"Do you want to eat with us?" I asked Kurt. He shook his head. I tried to talk him round, but he was already halfway out the door.

"I'm pleased to have met you," he said to Meisis and bowed in front of her. She laughed and waved at him through the window as he walked back into the forest.

Edith sat at the kitchen table, felt in the pocket of her coat and pulled out her lipstick. While Meisis laid the table and I served the soup, she painted her mouth. It was a glowing red that she hadn't used for a long time.

While we ate, no one said a word. Edith ate so slowly that she still wasn't finished after Meisis and I had already eaten two portions. I sent Meisis to bed, cleared away our dishes in the sink and was just about to go upstairs when Edith said: "Kurt has discovered something."

I didn't say anything. Edith put her spoon down and handled a piece of potato with her fingers.

"He spoke to people in the territory, and two of them saw something very interesting. They told Kurt, completely independently of one another, that shortly before Eggert's daughters disappeared, they saw them at the river. And both people concluded that it was as if they were teaching each other how to swim," Edith said, wiping her greasy fingers down her coat.

"What are you trying to tell me?" I asked.

Edith pushed back a strand of hair that had come loose from her bun, lifted her dish to her mouth, and drank the rest of the soup.

"Eggert's daughters wanted to cross the river. And they did

it, otherwise their bodies would have been found a long time ago, like with Ove and Nuuel. That means we could do it too."

"We've got a roof over our heads, a garden. No one knows what's left in the territories along the coast." As I continued to speak, my voice got louder. "You fled from there."

Edith looked at me, surprised.

"Yes, Kurt told me the whole story. How you climbed up the bank dripping wet. And you've not really concealed your origins, what with the pictures in your wardrobe."

Edith shrugged. "It's been many years since I fled. Who knows what it looks like there now?"

I couldn't believe that Edith was being serious. She reached for my hand. I flinched.

"If something miraculous doesn't happen, Pesolt and the others will come for Meisis. You won't be able to stop it. But if we go now, there's a chance that we three will survive."

"We would be leaving everything behind."

Edith's expression darkened. "What exactly do you mean by that?"

"Gösta and Len, they need me."

"They're old women, they'll be dead soon. That's what you want to risk your life for, Meisis's life?"

"They've always been there for me and took care of me. Unlike you."

"You didn't want me to look after you."

"Because you couldn't do it."

"Now you're exaggerating."

"If Gösta and Len hadn't have been there I would have starved."

"You were old enough. You had the rabbits, the potato patch."

"And you still don't get why I trust the territory more than you? You really have no idea about reality and that's why I will, under no circumstances, engage with your crazy idea about leaving. I know that you can't comprehend it, but the territory is my home."

Edith jumped up. Her stool fell with a loud bang.

"Your home," she shouted. "Have you forgotten all the things people did to you here? All the injuries. And then there's the loathing they show us here. Your home has treated you like the scum of the earth."

I jumped up too.

"It's about the land, not the people," I yelled. "How many times do I have to tell you?"

Red blotches were showing on Edith's face.

"Then stay in this godforsaken territory and perish" she shouted, "but I'm getting away from here, and I'm taking the child with me."

"You have my father on your conscience, and now you want to take the child away from me too?"

Edith starred at me, stunned. "What did you say?"

"You heard," I replied.

"So that's what you think of me?" Edith asked. "Then it really is better you stay here."

She staggered out of the room. I kicked her chair with full force. It flew against the wall and splintered with a crash.

I WOULD LIKE TO TAKE MY MOTHER'S BODY, POSITION IT IN THE DUSTY SAND AND DO LAPS OVER IT WITH THE PICK-UP.

63.

The next morning, I drove to Gösta and Len. It was oppressively hot; the sky was slightly hazy. I walked around the house and went into the garden. Gösta was wearing a tracksuit and was watering the onion beds, while Len was sleeping on a lounger in the shade. The hens were perched around as if guarding her.

"Len fell over in the kitchen this morning," Gösta said, following my gaze.

"Is she alright?"

"All things considered. She's very sullen about the weather. The warmer it gets, the more she'll lose her balance. She feels like the whole world's against her. More and more things she used to do alone she needs help for. It's gnawing at her, of course it is," Gösta said, adjusting her headscarf and reaching for the watering can next to her, yet her hand was shaking so much, she couldn't lift it.

"Let me do that," I said, picking up the watering can.

After the work we ate a dish of cold onion soup together on the terrace. Len had woken up and was sitting next to us, but when Gösta wanted to give her something to eat, she shook her head.

We talked about trivial things, and I tried to talk myself into thinking it was like it was before, a completely normal day, with nothing to fear. But the dark feeling didn't go away.

Once we'd finished eating, they pushed a bag of onions into my hands.

"You better have them," I tried to talk them out of it. But Gösta and Len insisted.

"For the child too," they said.

I thanked them. They walked me to the pick-up. Gösta had to support Len the whole way, it hurt me to see her like that.

"Don't worry about us. We're hardier than we look," Len said, laughing, but I knew that her nonchalance was just a front.

"I'll be back soon," I promised.

Gösta nodded. I got in the pick-up and drove off.

On the way back I saw three cherry plum trees heavy with fruit at the side of the road. In the last few years, they had only bloomed. I slowed down, drove up close to them and made up my mind to come back the next day with Meisis to harvest the trees.

I WANT TO SEE THE FULL TREES AS A GOOD OMEN.

Cherry plums always remind me of a particularly wonderful day with Gösta and Len. They took me to two trees near the river. At the crack of dawn, we shook the fruit from the branches and gathered them in large baskets.

In the house we washed the plums and decanted them into all the available pots. While Len and I pitted the fruit and sorted them, I threw the worm-eaten ones into a bucket under the table, Gösta cooked jam. The sweet smell made the air sticky. We were busy well into the evening. When the sun began to set, I made a move to leave, but Gösta pushed me back down onto my chair.

"No child should walk home in the dark," she said, "you'll sleep here tonight."

She fetched a blanket and a pillow and set up the sofa for

me. For the first time in a long while, I felt looked after. I slept deeply and dreamt of rain watering the landscape.

For a long time, the memory of this day helped me in my darkest hours.

64.

Early the next morning, even before the sun had completely come up, Meisis and I drove back to the spot. The vibrant yellow and red of the plums was accentuated by the luminous blue sky behind them. I parked the pick-up in a ditch, and we took the plastic buckets I'd fetched from the shed before we'd set off from the truck bed. We walked down the road towards the trees. The heavy scent of the almost overripe fruit hung in the air. I could hear the buzz of insects.

"Watch out for the wasps," I told Meisis, as she climbed up the trunk of one of the trees. I went over to the other tree. A lot of the fruit was already lying on the ground and rotting. I began filling the bucket. Soon my hands were sticky from the juice. When it was full, I took it over to the pick-up and put it on the bed. I took another bucket and went back. Meisis had climbed right to the top and was picking them from up there. She grinned down to me, her mouth smeared with juice.

"Picking, not eating," I called up to her.

I was just reaching for the second bucket when a shot rang out.

"Get away from those trees," shouted Pesolt, who came running over the field. He was only wearing rough jeans, no shirt. Across his belly was a red, glinting scar. Meisis dropped her bucket in fright. The plums spread all over the grass.

"They're not your trees," I shouted, and stood protectively in front of Meisis, who had quickly climbed down to me.

"The trees are on my land, I'm not letting the devil frolic in them," Pesolt spat at us. He must have been drinking. I could smell the alcohol, and his movements were laboured.

I gulped and remembered how he had once broken my nose after I had cut nettles on a field that was also on his land.

He had taken my skull in both his hands and had slammed it multiple times against the hot hood of my pick-up, so that the blood had shot right out of my nose and adorned a considerable part of the truck's white paintwork.

He only seemed calmer now because he was so drunk he could barely walk straight. He screwed up his eyes and tried to focus them on us.

"The plums stay here," he slurred, pointing at the bucket.

I looked at him wrathfully and tipped the fruit into the ditch.

"You can pick them yourself," I said.

He didn't let me out of his sight. I threw the buckets back onto the truck bed and pushed Meisis into the passenger seat.

"We're coming to get you soon," Pesolt called, pointing at Meisis. "And woe be to you if anything happens to my trees."

I got in behind the steering wheel. Pesolt leaned in towards us.

"I see that the child still has all its teeth. I'm counting down the days. If I catch you here again before then, I'll shoot you right out the tree. Then our little party will happen a bit earlier than planned."

He had spoken so quietly that Meisis couldn't have heard him. I quickly turned the key in the ignition and put my foot on the accelerator. Pesolt had to jump back so he wouldn't be carried along by car. In the side mirror I saw him standing in the road flailing his arms, getting smaller and smaller.

"I still saved a handful," Meisis said, reaching into the breast pocket of her dress and showing me five plums.

I tried to smile.

"We'll eat them when we get home," I said, and looked back at the highway.

Back at the house, we sat on the sofa in Meisis's room. She spread out a cloth handkerchief between us and lay the five plums on top of it.

"You can have three, I'll have two," she said, pushing the fruit towards me.

"You take three."

I gave her one back and put a plum in my mouth. It was so ripe that it liquified on my tongue. I spat the stone into my hand.

'Delicious, right?" Meisis looked at me. I nodded at her, and yet before my inner eye I saw the plums rotting on the trees.

Later, while Meisis was outside in the garden sorting my building blocks, I beat my fist multiple times against the wall in the attic. I beat it so hard the skin broke.

In the bathroom, I washed the blood from my knuckles and avoided looking myself in the eye in the mirror over the sink.

"What happened to your hand," Edith asked me as we passed each other in the hallway that night. In order to cool the bruised bone, I had wrapped a wet cloth around it.

I leaned against the handrail on the stairs and didn't respond.

Edith twisted her mouth in a mocking way. "You always want to sit things out and hope that everything sorts itself out in the end."

I shrugged my shoulders and went to bed.

65.

SOMETHING IS SLIDING, AND IT FEELS LIKE A DOWNWARD MOTION, I DON'T KNOW WHICH WAY TO SHOOT.

The next morning, Edith was gone. I couldn't find her in the house or in the garden, and her furs weren't anywhere to be found. I hoped she would never reappear.

But when she was standing among the pines around midday and then walked towards the house, I was actually relieved. Her eyes were tired, the seam of her dress was wet. Leaves hung from her coat.

"Where were you this morning?" I asked her when she was standing in the darkened kitchen that evening. She poured herself a glass of elderberry juice that I'd left out on the table and said: "I just did a couple of laps, it clears my head."

"I don't buy it," I said.

Edith shrugged her shoulders.

I took a few steps towards her and planted myself in front of her. "I haven't forgotten our argument. What are you not telling me?"

"Don't worry, I won't take the child away from you," Edith said, ducking around me and leaving the kitchen.

In the days that followed, she was sometimes gone for hours. She evaded my questions.

She got up every morning before us. When I came downstairs, she was already in front of the sink in the kitchen. She had started eating regularly again, wore a different dress every day and wore make-up. After breakfast, she put on lipstick and powdered her face.

It looked like a mask.

At the time it seemed to me that she was steeling herself for something.

That in a way she was, I only understood in retrospect.

Every evening she combed her hair with the brush made of driftwood.

When Meisis asked her, she braided her two plaits.

"What have they got against this colour?" she said, looking in wonder at the luminous copper tone. I watched both of them from the door. There was a throbbing behind my forehead. They didn't notice me, and I turned and left. I fetched the axe from the shed. I went deep into the forest and hacked at a branch that Meisis had recently pulled out of the undergrowth and that had been lying in her room ever since. I hacked at it for as long as it took for there to be almost nothing left of it. And yet I still couldn't fight the scenario incessantly repeating in my head: how I had once asked Edith for braids. In reply, she had said: "The straw on your head is much too unruly, it's impossible to do something good with it." She eyed me up snidely in the mirror of the dresser where she sat twisting her own shiny wet hair around driftwood and pinning it up. I bolted out of the room and put three of her books in my bag. I walked into the forest that very night, where I burned them in a clearing.

I never asked her again.

At dinner Edith now often held out her dish for a second helping, and she drank the juice from the jars of plums in the cellar. I watched her with suspicion. Our supplies dwindling.

"What are you playing at?" I asked her, after I caught her spooning mashed potatoes into her mouth in the bath. She avoided my look, acting all innocent.

"First you get upset that I don't eat enough, and now suddenly you're complaining when I do eat," she moaned.

I tensed my shoulders. "That doesn't mean you can just help yourself to the supplies whenever you want without thinking of us."

Edith nodded, but the next day I found her and Meisis laughing while they drank the last cartons of evaporated milk in the cellar. I ripped them out of their hands angrily.

"What did I say to you yesterday?" I shouted. Meisis looked at the freezer cabinet next to her guiltily. Edith withdrew to the sofa to brood.

When Edith and Meisis went to sleep that evening, I locked the pantry door and the hatch to the cellar and threaded both keys on a piece of string. I wore them around my neck from then on. Edith didn't bother asking for the keys.

66.

Even though it was a waste of petrol, I sometimes drove around the territory without a purpose. I needed a little space between myself and the house, where Meisis and Edith spent more and more time together. Driving fast and smoking helped me to reign in my anger at Edith. I hoped that a plan would come to me for how I could finally take Meisis out of the line of fire, because not a single tooth was loose yet.

On one of the days I was driving in the pick-up, I drove by Pesolt's cherry plum trees. As I passed them, I noticed that there was already new fruit on the branches. They were for the most part still green, but some were already nearly ripe. Twice in such a short amount of time. For as long as I could remember, that had never happened before. I drove on, preoccupied.

Later, as I lay in the garden and Meisis played among the cherry and plum trees, I wrote on a sheet of paper:

THE CHERRY PLUM TREES BEARING FRUIT AGAIN
SEEMS LIKE A TRAP TO ME.

In the night I dreamt of overripe fruit that burst when I touched them. Their fermenting scent saturated the ground, the air. The only sound was the buzzing of the wasps. Flies and hornets too. An unceasing flickering, a teeming, nothing stayed in place. I woke from my dream in terror. The close air was almost unbearable. It hummed with electricity, like right before a storm. I couldn't sleep for a long time and listened to the outside, but rainfall didn't come, and, at some point, I dozed off.

When I got up the next morning, the ground was as dry as it had been the evening before.

67.

Three days later, my suspicions were confirmed. I found out where Edith disappeared to so often.

It was midday when I happened to see her walk through the garden in the direction of the forest. I told Meisis to stay hidden in the attic and followed Edith.

I kept the distance between us so great she couldn't hear my steps, but I didn't let her out of my sight. We walked like this for a while through the forest. Finally, we arrived at the river. Mosquitos danced over the water. Behind it stood the concrete bridge like an indented cliff in the landscape. I was dizzy from the heat.

Edith carefully climbed down the bank, holding tightly onto the high grass so she wouldn't lose her balance. When she reached the bottom, she took off her shoes and stepped into the water. At this point of the river, it only came up to her ankles. The hem of her dress guzzled up the water. She stood like that for a while, then leaned down, put her hand in the water and bathed her neck and face. A dragonfly hovered motionlessly in the air above her head. Edith removed her dress and lay it next to the coat on the rocks. Underneath, she wore her mother-of-pearl-coloured bathing suit. Her body was much more muscular that I remembered. She waded into the water. The waves sloshed against her knees at first, then against her hipbones and finally against her chest. Her bright hair, that she had tied into a knot, shone in the sun. The water reflected the light too. She tentatively swam a few strokes, quickened her pace and gasped for breath. The current was strong, she had to fight against it. Her progress was slow. She arrived at the middle of the river, stopped and swam back, always cautious not to be wrenched away. The water washed her back onto the bank, where she got up shiny and wet and from there went back to the rocks where her dress and coat were. She made a contented face, stretched, got dressed and turned to leave. Before she could discover me, I ducked behind a tree.

I made the decision to confront her the following day.

EDITH IS BECOMING MORE AND MORE SURE IN THE WATER, SHE SWAM LIKE A PIECE OF WOOD, WITHOUT SINKING EVEN ONCE.

68.

Early the next morning, I went to the quarry. I smoked five cigarettes on the way, even though the pack was almost empty.

I stopped up on the edge. Wolf and Levke had left behind their schnapps bottles between the scrap cars. In one spot there was wood that had been bleached by the sun. In another, there was gravel formed into a pile. I recalled that it was me who had piled up these stones. I had spent an afternoon doing it because I didn't want to go home, where Edith had been lying motionless on the sofa for days and hadn't even reacted when I had put my hand right in front of her face.

As I was about to light a sixth cigarette, I noticed there was someone standing on the other side of the quarry. It was a girl, a little younger than me. She was wearing overalls that looked like they were made of paper. But the most remarkable thing about her was her hair. It was as red as Meisis's. She had seen me too. We stared at each other across the pit, then she turned on her heel and disappeared into the forest behind her. My heart was hammering. I blinked. There was no longer anything to indicate that the girl had really existed. I quickly ran down the slope and almost fell, I was just about able to brace myself. I rushed through the quarry and climbed back up the other side. There, I looked for the spot where I had seen the girl standing, but she hadn't left anything behind. Not even an imprint in the moss. I fought my way through the thicket lying behind it, yelled into the forest, listened. But no one answered me.

THE CONSTANT HEAT MAKES ME HALLUCINATE.

69.

I DREAMT OF THE RIVER. WATER WAS ALL AROUND ME. I WAS FREEZING, WITHOUT BEING ABLE TO SAY WHERE I WAS. I DIDN'T SEE THE RIVERBANK ANYWHERE. AND THEN A SHOT. IT CUT THROUGH THE DEPTHS, CUT THROUGH THE DREAM. I WOKE WITH A START.

I had fallen asleep at the kitchen table. The ceiling light was burning. Meisis was sitting opposite me and was drawing crosses with a pen on a sheet of paper. I ran my hand over my face and propped myself up.

"Did you hear that?" I asked.

She nodded hesitantly and said, "It sounded like something shattering." She turned the paper over and began to draw on the reverse side too.

"Where's Edith?" I asked, rubbing my eyes. I hadn't seen her since getting back from the quarry that afternoon.

Meisis shrugged. "She was pacing next to the brambles."

I got up and went to the window, but it was so dark I could only see my own face in the glass. I turned, went into the hallway, stepped out of the house and called Edith's name into the night, yet received no reply. For a moment I stayed outside, listening, but the landscape was quiet, quiet like I'd seldom experienced.

When I returned to Meisis in the kitchen, I said to her that it was time to go to bed. She reluctantly folded the sheet of paper, pocketed it and followed me into the bathroom. We brushed our teeth standing in front of the mirror. I noticed for the first time that the dark circles under my eyes were just as shadowy as Edith's. The exhaustion was even written on

Meisis's face. She rinsed her mouth out and showed me her teeth.

"Are any of them wobbly?"

She shook her head.

I opened the window in Meisis's bedroom. Not a sound came in from outside. Meisis made herself comfortable on the sofa bed. She had recently started placing the things she'd found during the day around her pillow. Today there were two pinecones, a twig she'd peeled the bark from, and three rowan berries. She pushed the drawing of the crosses under her pillow.

"You'll stay until I've fallen asleep, won't you?" she asked. I nodded, turned off the light and sat on the floor next to the sofa. I leaned my back against the wall. From the corridor a small slit of light pushed under the door. The sight soothed me, but when I closed my eyes, I once more saw the dividing mass of water, so I stared into the dark room, where the contours of the furniture swam.

70.

Later, while I was washing our dishes, I heard someone whistling outside. I went to the window and looked out. Underneath the light over the door stood Wolf. He looked in an even worse state than last time. I took a knife from the sideboard and stepped out to him.

"What do you want?" I asked in a hushed voice. The situation seemed surreal to me.

Under his cap he was as pale as a lime washed wall. He nervously wiped his sweaty palms down his trousers and said: "We hit someone."

"What are you talking about?"

"We hit someone with the car," he said. Wolf took off his cap and twisted it in his hands.

"But you don't have a car."

Wolf and Levke used to race their cars down the highway at night for fun. It didn't take even a year before they put their cars into a tree and were lucky that that was all they'd done. The bruises, cuts, their damaged bodies, they had put it all on show afterwards, as if they had been wounded in a significant battle.

No one had wanted to lend them a car since, so they had to walk everywhere on foot, or they rode together on one bicycle. One on the saddle, the other on the rack. But in the last few years, they had often been too drunk even for that.

"Levke and I," Wolf stuttered, "we borrowed Pesolt's car. We do that sometimes, when Pesolt's drunk too much, because then he usually sleeps a few days and doesn't even know."

I didn't understand what Wolf was getting at. I stepped impatiently from one foot to the other.

"What's that got to do with me?" I asked. "Who did you hit?"

Wolf's eyes widened. "A girl," he said.

"What girl?" I became impatient. "Wolf, what are you talking about?"

He chewed his lower lip. "She wasn't from here," he said.

"What do you mean, she wasn't from here?"

"She has red hair."

I held my breath.

"Like the child," he added.

"Where is she now?"

"Who?"

"Damn it, the girl that you hit?"

Wolf rubbed his hands down his trousers again.

"Spit it out."

"In the trunk of Pesolt's car."

I cursed. "Take me to her."

Wolf didn't move.

"Right now," I shouted.

Wolf lead me through the forest. I couldn't say how long we walked for, but it felt like an eternity. It didn't seem to take any effort for Wolf to orientate himself in the darkness, while I no longer knew in which cardinal direction we were going within only a few metres.

Pesolt's car was standing in the middle of the road. Levke was leaning against the hood. When she saw us, she cursed. "What took you so long?" Just like Wolf, she seemed to still be in a state of shock.

"I want to see her," I said.

Levke led me around the car and opened the trunk.

It was the girl from the quarry. Her hair glowed red. She had a cut on her forehead. I bent over her. On her wrist shimmered a mother-of-pearl bracelet. It was the one I'd placed on the tree stump. My heart began to beat faster. I reached for her arm, felt her wrist and took a step back.

"She's still alive," I said.

Wolf rushed to my side. "Are you sure?"

"I can feel her pulse."

Levke pushed Wolf aside and gripped the girl's wrist herself. "Skalde's right."

"What do we do now?" Wolf asked, pacing up and down.

"We'll bring her to our house before someone sees us," I said. It briefly went black in front of my eyes. I had to steady myself against the car.

Wolf touched my shoulder. "Are you okay?" I pushed his hand away.

"Yes, I'm fine."

I pushed myself off of the car, opened the door and shuffled onto the backseat. Levke got in front of the wheel, Wolf sat in the passenger seat. When I looked out of the window, I saw a cat in the undergrowth. Its white fur filthy. It seemed to notice me looking at it. The car drove off, I wrenched my head in the cat's direction and watched as it ducked and disappeared into the forest.

We drove without lights. No one said anything. When we reached the house, I was the first to get out. I opened the trunk.

"You have to help me carry her into the house," I said, cradling the girl's upper body, Levke took her legs, and together we carried her through the door that Wolf held open for us and laid her on the sofa in the living room. I checked the girl's pulse. I could still make out a faint heartbeat.

"And now?" Wolf and Levke asked, looking at me.

"The car, you have to take it back to Pesolt."

They nodded, but didn't make a move to leave. I stood up and pushed them to the door.

"I can deal with this, hurry, before Pesolt wakes up."

They finally pulled themselves together.

As they drove off, I closed the door and turned the key in the lock. I leaned exhausted against the wood.

Meisis came downstairs. She looked at me sleepily.

"Did you go out?" she asked, rubbing her eyes.

I crouched down in front of her and pulled her towards me.

"There's someone in the living room," I said, "but you mustn't be afraid."

I took her by the hand and lead her in. When she saw the redhaired girl, she tore herself away from me and rushed towards the sofa.

"What's wrong with her?" Meisis asked.

"She had an accident. But she's alive."

I crouched down next to her and wanted to know from her who the girl was.

Meisis pressed her lips together.

"Tell me everything you know right now."

"Metta."

"What?"

"That's my sister, Metta."

I had to sit down. "Your sister? But why is she here? Where did she come from?"

"She was here the whole time."

"Here in the territory?"

Meisis's nod was reluctant. "She hid. She's good at hiding. No one's as good at hiding as Metta."

"You knew she was here the whole time?"

"It was Metta's idea. I wanted to hide, but I was always found. And our supplies were all gone. Metta said I had to be found, so I could eat properly again, so I would be able to keep going with her."

"Keep going where?"

"To the sea. Away from the hear.

Everything's burnt in the place where we came from."

"You managed to flee out of the dead territory?"

"Metta knew that we couldn't stay there. She knew before anyone and then we set off on our own because no one would listen to us."

"The others stayed?"

Meisis nodded.

"Why did you want to go to the sea?" I asked.

"Metta said that everything will burn here too."

"Our territory is safe," I said insistently.

Meisis shook her head.

"But the sick animals come from the sea. They're fleeing from there," I said.

"Metta says that the sea is our last chance."

I got up. I felt dizzy, almost as if I had lost my balance.

"I have to find Edith," I said, leaving the living room. I went up to the second floor and tried to open Edith's bedroom door. It was locked. I tried pulling down the handle again, but it wouldn't open. I called Edith's name and knocked. I heard no sound from the hallway.

The crowbar was hanging on the wall in the shed. I took it off its hook and went back upstairs. I needed the briefest moment to pry open the door.

The light was burning, illuminating the room. I approached the wardrobe mirror and faced myself. My gaunt body didn't feel like it was my own. Lips dry and cracked. The sun had further bleached my hair. Freckles like dirt on my skin. For the first time, I thought I resembled Edith.

I carefully opened the wardrobe doors. The roller suitcase with inside. I pulled it out. It couldn't be empty; it was too heavy for that. I lay it on the bed and opened it. A few of Edith's dresses were carefully arranged inside it, and a bag of her jewellery, as well as the white fur coat for Meisis. I took all of it out, right at the bottom I found two t-shirts and a pair of trousers that belonged to me. Something shifted in my ribcage. Edith had packed to flee. After everything that had happened, she had held onto the idea that all three of us would be going together. I could clearly picture how hopefully she had packed everything in the suitcase. I had to turn away. My throat tightened.

"Have you found Edith?" Meisis asked me when I came downstairs. I shook my head.

"She must be taking a walk," I said, trying not to sound afraid.

71.

I felt feverish. I sat up feeling dazed. The light fell brightly into the room. The sun must have just come up. I got up and went downstairs. Edith's room was unchanged. I opened the bathroom door; the tub was empty. The kitchen, too, showed no indication that Edith had returned.

I fetched onions from the pantry, cut them into large pieces and slid them into a pot. While I was pouring water into it, I heard a meowing. I went to the window and looked outside. Next to the pool, a cat was sitting in the grass, looking towards the house and emitting high plaintive cries.

"We should let it into the house," said Meisis, who had appeared in the doorway. "She's looking for Metta."

I reluctantly agreed. Meisis opened the back door. The cat pushed passed her legs and went into the living room.

"She helped Metta hide," Meisis told me.

"The cat?"

She nodded. I turned back to the soup and stirred it. Without looking up, I said: "Why didn't you tell me the truth?"

Meisis didn't reply. I put the lid on the pot and turned to her.

"I'd like to know right now."

"Metta said I couldn't tell anyone about her."

"Not even me?"

"I was scared."

"Scared of what?"

"That you would tell the others about her."

I looked at her, wounded by what she'd said.

"I'm sorry."

I wanted to take the pot off of the stove, but my hands were shaking too much.

"You used me," I said.

"That's not true," Meisis protested, but I didn't want to hear it.

"I have to go find Edith," I said, pushing passed her and going into the garden. The sunlight was so harsh it hurt my eyes. I fled into the forest, kept walking, barely taking notice of the way I was taking. I only found the clearing by chance. There it was, undisturbed. I stepped out from between the trees. Within the circular area the scent of the pine forest thickened. That's how it always had been, that was why I built my den here. In this clearing, I felt closest to the forest.

"Skalde?" I heard Meisis calling. I didn't respond. Blood was rushing in my ears. Meisis stepped out from behind a tree. The only thing between us was the clearing. We looked at one another. It felt like years had passed since the last time we had been standing here.

"Never lie to me again, you hear," I shouted.

Meisis nodded and came over to me. I stayed where I was.

"I promise," she said when she'd reached me. She held my gaze.

"Good," I said, and after a long pause: "Let's go back to the house."

As we entered the living room, Metta was conscious. She was sitting up on the sofa. In her lap was the cat, purring. Metta didn't seem surprised to see us. I remained wavering in the doorway.

"How are you feeling?" Meisis asked, crouching down by her sister.

"Did I have an accident?" Metta asked. Meisis nodded.

"You're safe here," I said, trying to smile. Metta reciprocated. "You should take it easy another couple of days. You probably have a concussion."

Metta held her head and felt the wound, where a scab had already formed. "Thank you," she said.

"I didn't do much."

"You took in Meisis."

"Yes," I said, and didn't know what to do with my hands.

72.

At noon, Edith still hadn't shown up. I was gripped by a strong feeling of unease. I paced back and forth. Metta had fallen asleep, and the cat was likewise dozing, but Meisis wasn't able to sit still. She was constantly lifting her head and looking at the door.

"I'm going to go look for Edith," I said, putting on my shoes.

Meisis jumped up. "I'll come with you."

"Don't you want to stay with Metta?"

She shook her head. "She's safe here in the house. I want to help you."

She went into the living room. Through the open door I could see her lean down to her sister and talk to her in whispers. The intimacy between them pained me, I couldn't deny it, and it made me feel ashamed.

The pick-up was in front of the house, where I had parked it the day before. There were squashed flies stuck to the windscreen. They reminded me of burst blackberries. I got behind the wheel. Meisis climbed into the passenger seat. She put her feet in the too-big trainers up on the dashboard. I folded down the sun visor, started the engine, and drove off.

It was a particularly hot day. I could feel the sweat running down my back underneath my t-shirt. Elderflower was in bloom all over the territory. The heavy buds hung rotting on the trees. Meisis had one arm out of the half-open window. The airstream churned her hair. A fly had flown in and was circling us, buzzing. I couldn't scare it away.

I was driving so slowly, I could look at the landscape

carefully both left and right. Meisis, too, twisted her head so nothing escaped her.

We turned into the road where the three cherry plum trees stood, and I knew it immediately. My stomach tightened. I blinked; water lunged before my closed eyelids. A shot reverberated. The pick-up got slower and slower. My hands went slack, we came to a stop right in front of the trees.

The noontime heat lay heavily over the land.

"Why are we stopping?" Meisis asked. I didn't give her an answer. My hands slipped from the steering wheel. I turned my head and looked through the rolled down window at the cherry plum trees. The fruit had become ripe in the meantime. Some of them were even already rotting, even though they were still hanging on the branches. The drone of the wasps drifted over to us. But other insects had also been lured by the tree. I could clearly make out a swarm of flies circling over a spot on the ground, rising from it over and over again, to then once more settle on it.

First, I noticed the dogs. They were cowering in the high grass in the shadow of the trees. There were a lot of them, they must have come from the surrounding farms.

I slowly opened the door. My body felt numb, yet I managed to put one foot in front of the other. I made my way over to the trees as if in a trance. From some place far away Meisis called after me. I didn't turn around, kept going towards the spot where the buzz of the flies was concentrated. The dogs didn't move, the only sign of stirring they showed was a deep growl, but it wasn't meant for me.

Edith's twisted body was almost invisible in the high grass. She was lying on her stomach. The black fur of her coat shimmered dully. Her light hair covered the ground like an open fan. The yellow and red cherry plums in their sweet juice all around her. Everything crawling. The buzz of the flies was overwhelming. I crouched down next to her and turned her body onto its back. Her face was as white as paper, her eyes rolled upwards. Blood crusted on her mouth. Blood on her stomach, her chest. Already dry. Three clearly identifiable bullet wounds. From her coat pocket poked the edge of a plastic bag. I pulled on it. It was filled with plums. Flies here too. I immediately dropped the bag.

I thought of the word PROVISIONS and saw before my inner eye Edith, Meisis and me swimming with this plastic bag through endless waters. The red and yellow of the fruit glowed. How we reached the other bank, dripping, the bag still in my hand, and how we climbed up the embankment and made off in the direction of the coast.

I blinked and felt for my throat, around which I still wore the keys to the cellar and the larder. The buzzing of the insects had slipped to a back section of my mind. I heard it as if I was under water. I wrapped my arms around Edith's body, lifted it up and carried it across the road to the pick-up. Meisis looked out of the window, chalk white. I heaved Edith onto the truck bed, tumbled to the front of the car and slid into the seat. The dogs had followed me, they had positioned themselves behind the truck. There must have been over twenty of them. As I drove off, they followed us. Meisis didn't make a sound. She sat as if petrified.

It felt like someone else was operating the accelerator, the clutch, the gearstick. The truck was driving itself, while I sunk further and further into my own body.

I came to with someone sprinkling water in my face. Gösta was bent over me. She lowered the hand holding the glass. It was shaking.

"Get out of the car," she said, opening the door. I pushed myself from the seat and slipped into her arms. She hauled me through the front garden, passed the dogs that were standing in a row next to the path to the house. The elderflower wasn't yet in bloom here. The scent appeared to have fallen out of time. As we were about to cross the threshold, I turned to the truck.

"Edith," I said, pointing at the truck bed, but it was empty.

"I know," Gösta gently pulled me onwards, "she's inside."

I tried to swallow, but I couldn't. My mouth was dust dry. Gösta brought me into the kitchen. Meisis was sitting at the table, behind her stood Len, resting her hands on the back of the chair. Blood was on her fingers. I fell into a chair opposite her. At the sink Gösta filled two glasses with tap water and put them down in front of us. I reached for one, but my hand slipped from it.

"What exactly happened?" Len asked. Meisis and I didn't say anything. I couldn't take my eyes off the glass of water.

"Damn it, girls, you have to talk to us," Gösta said.

I tried once more to reach for the glass, this time I managed it. In a motion that seemed to last an eternity, I led it to my mouth. I took a sip and put it back down.

"She must have climbed the tree," I said, "to pick plums."

Len's forehead rumpled.

"They're Pesolt's trees. He shot her," I said.

I wanted to take another sip from the glass, but my hands failed. I folded them in my lap.

"Pesolt didn't really do this?"

"A couple of weeks ago Meisis and I were there and tried to harvest them. He had threatened to shoot us if he saw us near his trees again."

Meisis wiped her wet face.

"My God," Gösta said, balling her wrinkled hands into fists. "Pesolt's gun used to be mine."

It took a moment before I understood what Gösta had said. "Your gun?" I asked.

"They wanted to pin stuff on me too. I handed the gun over to Pesolt. He's had his eye on it for a while, I knew that. That's how I could convince him to finally leave us alone."

"You gave Pesolt your weapon?"

"We had no other choice," Len jumped in to Gösta's aid.

"I vouched for the child, remember? If I hadn't done that, I would never have had to have given him anything."

I sank back down in my chair. "Sorry," I said.

Gösta nodded. "You're right. But I would never have thought he would use the gun."

I stared at the grain of the table. "Where's Edith now?" I asked.

Gösta made a head motion towards the living room. "We've laid her on the sofa."

I nodded and got up.

"Where are you going?" I asked.

"To get Edith, and then we're going home." I answered decisively.

"Wouldn't you rather stay here?" Len asked. "What's there for you at the house?"

"Edith has to be buried,"

"That can wait," Gösta stood in my way. "Stay. No one will suspect you're here."

"We're not safe anywhere anymore. Not even here," I said, giving Meisis a sign that we were going. She jumped up and took my hand. Together we pushed past Gösta and Len into the hallway.

The light in the living room was diffuse. On the television

was the same recording that I'd watched with Gösta months before. It seemed unfamiliar to me now. Edith's dead body was laid out on the sofa. I bent over her and lifted her up. She was light. It made me think of driftwood. I carried her through the narrow hallway. Meisis walked ahead of me and opened the front door. The sunlight dazzled me. I screwed up my eyes and staggered down the stairs. I lay Edith on the truck bed. Her mouth was slightly open. Blood shimmered on her teeth.

"Take this at least," called Gösta. She rushed out the house and handed me a blanket. Together we wrapped Edith's corpse inside it. Meisis stood silently nearby.

"Be careful," Gösta said as a farewell.

I wanted to shake her hand, but she took a step towards me and hugged me. I could feel every bone through her clothes. She pulled Meisis to her too. Len stepped through the door and came over to us.

"Chins up," she said.

I kissed her on both cheeks, and we got into the pick-up. As we drove off, they waved after us. The dogs followed us, barking.

73.

We found the house just as we had left it. Meisis helped me to carry Edith's dead body inside.

"When it's dark, I'll start digging a grave," I said, standing in the kitchen in front of the window. The dogs sat in the shade of the house and didn't stir. The water in the pool had turned brown. The surface lay so undisturbed that the sky was reflected in it. I tried to imagine that Edith was swimming in it, but the water remained still.

I stood at the window until the sun went down. The shadows grew longer, and the blue became lost in the black.

Outside, the dogs greeted me. They followed me to the shed, from where I fetched the shovel, and walked behind me to the lilac bush in front of the house. There I began to dig a grave. My movements were mechanical. The numbness had returned. If I closed my eyes, I saw the cascading mass of water. The shot was now clearly audible. Around me, the dogs dozed.

Metta and Meisis came outside. They brought me a torch and helped me to dig. We worked in silence. All that could be heard was the sound of the shovel in the dry earth. The sweat made our clothes stick to us. Time and time again, Meisis went to the pump and fetched water, which we hastily drank. We didn't take a break.

It took till sunrise. The hole was around a meter and a half deep. Smeared with earth, we stood there while the sun rose over the pine forest.

Together with Metta I fetched Edith's corpse from the house and we lowered her on the sheet into the bottom of the pit. We lay her jewellery and her clothes into the grave too, her swimsuit last of all.

Someone whistled, we turned. Out of the forest came Kurt. Under his rabbit fur coat, he was wearing a crumpled suit. His face was serious, he nodded at us. I was going to say something, but he shook his head.

He just said: "I know."

"What do people say at funerals?" I asked him.

Metta and Meisis lowered their heads.

"That's up to you."

"I looked at him helplessly.

"Maybe something Edith liked," he said. "Wait a moment."

He went into the house and came back a short time later. In his hand he was holding a slim book with a worn cover. He gave it to me. I opened it and recognised the poems. Edith had known them all off by heart. With my shoulders back, I stood at the fresh grave and read to Edith in a low voice.

When I stopped speaking, a soft silence spread. The sky was dark blue, like water that's a hundred metres deep.

I DREAMT THAT THE RIVER ROSE AND BROKE ITS BANKS. FIRST IT FLOODED THE FOREST, THEN THE MEADOWS, FINALLY THE HOUSES.
THE TERRITORY SILENTLY WENT UNDER.
I DREAMT I WENT SWIMMING IN THIS WATER. I WORE EDITH'S WHITE SWIMSUIT AND SWAM WITH EVEN STROKES, THE SUNKEN LANDSCAPE FAR BENEATH ME, AND AS I REACHED THE MIDDLE OF THE RISEN SEA, I NOTICED THAT THE WATER TASTED SALTY.

I woke up and didn't know where I was. The light had no permanence. I rubbed my eyes. Earth was stuck to my hands. I managed to focus my eyes and sit up. I had slept beside the grave. The dogs were gone. A heavy scent lay in the air. I turned towards the lilac bush, among the fleshy leaves bright violet blossoms had burst open. It was the first time in years. I lay down and decided to never get up again.

74.

The days that followed now seem to me, looking back, strangely distorted. I can't remember if I actually slept, only individual scenes stand clearly before my eyes, what happened between them has disintegrated.

I remember Meisis wore the white rabbit fur coat that Edith had sewn for her. She sat like a snow hare in the shade of the house, out in the garden, in spite of the heat.

I remember Metta crouching among the books in the living room and Meisis reading a fairy tale where seven brothers disappear, while I lay on the carpet and drew patterns on the ceiling with my eyes.

I remember Kurt cooking onion soup in the kitchen and feeding the child because it couldn't move its arms, and giving me some of the soup and speaking quietly to me.

I remember standing at the window in the kitchen and watching the sun come up, and then closing my eyes, and when I opened them again it was evening, and the darkness was drawing in over the landscape.

I remember Metta and Meisis sitting with me in Edith's wardrobe and, using the torch, we looked at the pictures of the sea, the radio between us, and we listened to the quiet rushing sound that ebbed away and then became louder, just as Edith had described the sound of the waves.

I remember us standing in the garden collecting empty snail shells in the last of the light and crushing them between stones, for hours, until we couldn't find anymore and our hands were all dusty.

I remember all of this, but maybe I only dreamt it.

75.

I woke with a start, gasping for air, as if I had just been under water. For the first time in a long time, I saw my surroundings clearly again. The sunlight cut sharp edges around the living room. I got up from the carpet.

I found Meisis and Metta in the kitchen, where they sat at the table looking at me with serious faces. At their feet, the cat was crouching and still. All I could hear was its purring.

"We're going to cross the river," Metta said, "before the people come and get us."

"What?"

"We can't wait any longer."

"If you try and cross the river you'll drown."

"I've been training. I can do it. With Meisis too."

"But you don't know what's waiting for you on the other side."

"We can't stay here. We have to try our luck."

"Come with us Skalde," Meisis said.

I stared out of the window. The garden lay there unchanged. I wished I could go into the pine forest. Lie flat on the ground and lose the feeling of my body.

After a long pause I said: "I can't."

"It's just a question of technique," Metta said, "I can teach you."

I shook my head. "The territory. I belong here."

"It will get even hotter here, you won't be able to stop it," Metta said.

I didn't respond and ran my finger over the grain of the sideboard. The cat jumped onto Meisis's lap and curled up. Its eyes narrowed into small slits.

"Skalde, please," Meisis said.

"I'll think about it," I said, turning around and going outside. In the front garden, the lilac bush was still in bloom. I stood so close to it, the scent was the only thing I could perceive.

TO LEAVE A FAMILIAR TERRITORY I COULD NAVIGATE BLIND.
WHAT LASTS, AND WHAT IS LEFT, IF I GO? WHO WILL REMEMBER THE PATH I LEAVE BEHIND?

76.

I drove with the pick-up to Gösta and Len. On the way I passed the cherry plum trees. Not a single fruit was hanging from the branches. As if it had never happened. I shook my head.

I reached the house and knew straight away that something had shifted. With a pounding heart I knocked on the door, but no one opened it. I tried pulling down the handle, the door wasn't locked.

Inside, I called their names, but received no answer. In the living room it smelled of sweat. The television was switched off. The kitchen looked like it had just been cleaned. Nothing was out of place. I leant over the sink and noticed the remnants of CELANDINE. Small yellow flowers and dark green leaves. That was probably when I was overcome by my first suspicion.

I stepped out the backdoor and walked through the heat to the vegetable garden. In the middle of the beds was the sun lounger. Gösta and Len were lying on it. They were holding one other, their eyes closed, but they weren't sleeping. That they had chosen their death had something peaceful about it, and yet nothing was as it should be anymore. I lost my balance, slipped, lay down. All I could see was the sky, the harmonious blue. I didn't move, and my gaze swam.

At some point I noticed a point high up above, a disturbance in the colour. The point got nearer, became larger. It was a seagull. It sank further and further down and circled over the garden; for a moment it hovered motionless in the sky. Then it let itself be carried back up on the air, climbed higher and higher and disappeared in a northerly direction, there, where the sea was. Till then, I had never believed in signs.

I stood, crouched down next to the dead women, said goodbye by touching their hands one last time.

In the house I looked for a message they might have left for me. What I found was a bag positioned in the middle of their bed. In it were two life jackets. Sewn together Styrofoam. Reflectors. In my head the image of the river appeared, the water no longer unbeatable. In the bag was also a video cassette. RECORDINGS OF THE TERRITORY. THE LAST YEAR, Len had written on white tape, and aside from that, a note: NO ONE HAS EVER MANAGED TO LEAVE.

I put everything back in the bag and left the house.

77.

The lilac had almost withered. In a few days, nothing would be left of the heavy flowers. I parked the pick-up next to the sand path, just as I always had, only this would be the last time. For a long while, I stared through the windscreen at the house. I tried to get a lasting impression of it, and yet I knew that I wouldn't be able to hold onto it in all its clarity.

I climbed out. The sand crunched beneath my feet. Before I opened the door, I touched the place where the paint was flaking off.

In the hallway, I picked up Edith's coat, which was lying on the tiles, and put it on. I met my defiant gaze in the mirror.

Meisis and Metta were sitting in the kitchen. It seemed like they hadn't moved since I'd left the house. Only the cat had gone. I stood before them and said: "Let's go."

I collected my notes. I really had hidden them all over the house and in every conceivable nook. I piled up the pieces of paper on the kitchen table. The years compressed into words and letters of the alphabet. I took the tin with my milk teeth, too. When I reached the window halfway up the stairs, I formed a gun with my left hand and aimed it at the evening sky. I whispered 'bang, bang.'

In the kitchen I bound the notes, the can with the teeth and the video cassette in a plastic bag to form a waterproof package. Meisis filled a rucksack with the food we still had left. Metta stood still.

On a piece of paper I wrote Kurt a message. If he wanted, he should live in the house. I placed the note in the middle of the table.

The last of the light made the trunks of the pines glow red. Meisis walked out. Under my sole the grass snapped, as if about to catch fire. Before stepping into the forest, I took one last look back. The sun was setting behind the house. The sky looked like it was burning. My heart was heavy while I said goodbye. It felt unimaginable to know that I would never be coming back. I nodded to the house one final time and stepped between the pines, stepped into the familiar scent of the trees, following Metta and Meisis. We took our time. Sometimes I paused and lay my hand on the cracked bark of a tree. If it had been possible to fold up the forest and keep it, I would have stowed it in my coat pocket.

The trees thinned out, we had reached the river. The water gleamed like black lacquer. The sight of the concrete bridge occupied a large part of the landscape.

A moth got caught in my hair. I freed it carefully and had to think of Gösta's butterfly collection. Would someone take them on? Or would everything just be lost? I forbade myself from thinking of it any longer.

We climbed down to the water and looked at the other side. Meisis and I put on the lifejackets.

You have to move like a frog, I heard Edith's voice in my head. I stuffed the plastic bag into the inside pocket of my coat.

Metta and Meisis looked at me.

We held hands. I hesitated for a moment, then I nodded, and we waded into the river. For a moment we felt the current. The further we went in, the more it tore at us.

"Don't let go of me," I shouted to Meisis. Then I began to swim. The world tipped, and the only thing I heard was the roar of the water. It received me, as if it had been waiting for me for years.